Exit Light
Jose Cantu

For Mom and Dad

There's a place you have seen
In your wild imaginings
Where who you are is the same
As who you've wanted
I Come to Shanghai – "Another Sunday Morning"

Exit Light

As Marco Serra turned the corner of the downtown street in the dead of night, the urge to light up a cigarette kicked in again. He hadn't been much of a smoker before. He didn't previously hate the habit, but he never really felt a need for it either. Lately however, the nicotine itch kept incessantly eating at him like bloodsucking fleas on a mangy dog. It was an itch he had to scratch. He reached into the inside pocket of his black leather jacket and pulled out a pack of Camel cigarettes.

Marco cupped the cheap plastic lighter over the cancer stick as he lit up and kept walking. The swirling winds were so strong that it was almost impossible to light the damn thing and smoke at all, but he needed the distraction that smoking provided him. Smoking always helped Marco clear his mind when it got muddled and it helped him calm down if he was pissed off. He was grateful about that. He would have to thank Claire for introducing him to his new vice. He thought of her as he walked.

Claire was one of a select number of people Marco could call a friend, though not reliably so. Claire had her own way of being his friend. She would sort of hang around sometimes, coming and going as she pleased, dropping by unannounced and then leaving again in a rush without much of an explanation. She was like a ghost in the night, here for a moment and gone the next. He knew better than to question her about it though; it wouldn't get him anywhere and it would only keep her away until she was sure he wouldn't ask again. That was just how she was, and though Marco didn't exactly like being kept in the dark, he enjoyed spending time with her too much to stop seeing her altogether.

Marco focused on his cigarette and tried putting Claire and anyone else out of his thoughts. There was really no point worrying about it. The weather had dropped dramatically and the biting wind wasn't helping any. Marco buttoned up his jacket and put his non-smoking hand in his pocket.

Damn it's cold. What the hell am I doing?

Here I am, he thought, *two-thirty Tuesday morning on a cold, windy night and I'm out for a leisurely stroll freezing my ass off and I don't even know why.*

All Marco knew was that he needed to get out of his apartment for a while. He needed to leave that place that was usually a comfort to him but for whatever reason now made him feel claustrophobic and almost like he was suffocating. He felt as if an apartment-sized coffin was closing in on him. He didn't know why it was so, but the feeling of unease was strong enough to almost physically drag him out of his cocoon that was his home. Most occasions, Marco would be absently content to watch his nights and days melt into each other. He would watch television in an almost vegetative state, barely registering what was actually showing. He would drink his Coors and think about plenty of things that he would like to do and end up doing none of them. TV shows would end and commence and he paid them no attention. It was all white noise. The only sense of movement and purpose were when Marco went to work at the recycling yard. There at least he was doing something. The physical work felt good and Marco never felt drowned by his own thoughts and the general ennui that owned most other times.

Most. With that, Marco thought about Claire again. Claire was anything but boring or lacking in spirit. Though Marco never really knew or could count on Claire to be there when he would ask for her, the moments that they did spend together were always memorable, even if not always cheerful. Claire could have a temper, sometimes lashing out at Marco without provocation. She would burst out of Marco's apartment, slamming the door and burning rubber on her motorcycle, leaving Marco wondering about what the hell had just happened. A day or two later she would usually call to apologize, though she wouldn't do so in person. Sometime after that - anywhere between a day or up to several weeks later - she would drop by and the two would get drunk at home or at a bar as if nothing had happened. And that's how it went.

A powerful gust of wind suddenly blew the cigarette out of Marco's mouth, snapping him out of his thoughts. Marco watched the cigarette take flight and swirl in the air for a few seconds before gravity and the dying of the wind brought it down to the dirty street next to him. He watched the Camel roll back to the sidewalk and the slowly fall into the gutter next to him, surely the resting place of many a cigarette butt. He thought of lighting a second smoke but decided against it. He shoved both of his freezing hands into his jacket pockets and raised the hoodie of his jacket to protect his head from the cold, and resumed his stroll. He considered the possibility that walking the downtown streets of Brownsville, Texas well past midnight, alone, might not be the safest or most sensible thing that he'd ever done, but he reasoned that anyone wanting to cause trouble probably wouldn't be hiding around a dark corner on a freezing night with the intent of ambushing a random passerby. Even the dumbest of delinquents had to have more sense than that. The main thing he had to worry about, he thought, would be a big stray dog with a big, bad temper. But he tried not to worry about that either.

Marco didn't know why of all the nights to want to go out for a stroll he chose this one. Out of all the warm nights in this subtropical city he had to choose the most unseasonably cold one to wander off to collect his thoughts, if in fact that was what he was doing. He couldn't put his finger on it, but there was an uneasy feeling compelling him to get up and get out that he couldn't ignore. A voice from nowhere nagged and nagged at him until his whole body had ached with it. Eventually, after sitting in front of the tube for several hours and pretending to watch one pointless program or another, Marco gave up trying to ignore the insistent voice in his head, got dressed and went out. It wasn't like he was going to get much sleep anyway. He got his jacket from the closet, picked up his keys from the coffee table in the living room and walked out the door. He didn't take his car; he didn't feel much like driving and didn't want to waste gas if he was only going to be gone for a short while. Besides, Marco thought more clearly during walks than while driving.

Several minutes and quite a walking distance later, still with no real destination or even a reason for going out on his stroll, Marco stopped walking and leaned against the cold concrete wall of one of the closed downtown stores. He spied a wood and metal bench a block away and went to it instead. He sat down heavily and looked around out of habit. He didn't really expect to see anyone. A few seconds after he sat down, however, a marked police car drove by right in front of him. Marco thought that surely the cop would question him about his business there and promptly shoo him away. But the cop passed him by without so much as slowing down or even looking his direction. Marco felt mildly insulted. *What if I needed help*? But he soon put that thought out of his mind. He bent down and rested his elbows on his legs and stared at the cold and dirty sidewalk. He glanced up and looked through the glass windows behind the aluminum mesh that protected the store. Porcelain figures and cheap paintings stared back at him through the mesh. He sat there for several minutes, shivering in the cold. He thought maybe he should return home right then but the calm whispering in his mind kept telling him no. Not yet. *Well, maybe I should just stay here until I freeze to death or get stabbed by a homeless guy!* He looked at his watch. It was a quarter past three in the morning. At least he didn't have to get up too early. He didn't have to be at work until 10:00 AM. Marco could function reasonably well with only a handful hours of sleep, but he didn't want to stay up until sunset for no reason either. He let out a loud, frustrated sigh, his cold breath materializing in the freezing air.

Right, I'm leaving, he thought. He got up and started walking back to his apartment. He hadn't realized how far he had gone until his walk back. It would take a good thirty minutes before he was back at home. At least moving would keep him a little warmer than sitting on that cold bench. As he was making his way down the lonely sidewalk, he casually glanced at the names of the buildings with the impossibly generic titles: Zapateria, Ropa Usada, Electronicos. Most of the buildings were one or two stories and all of them were ancient. Marco didn't like it there. There was something about these buildings and this part of town that he found depressing, like something trapped in the past. Not that the rest of Brownsville itself was a beacon of modernity, but at least the rest of the city seemed to be making an effort to not look two-hundred years old, or however old the city actually was. Brownsville was neither a small town nor a giant city like Houston, but somewhere in between, the border of Mexico a spitting distance from downtown. On the Border by the Sea indeed.

There was one building in this time-forsaken part of the city that Marco did like seeing, however. He had always enjoyed, on the rare occasion that he found himself downtown, driving by a two-story building called The Majestic. The Majestic was once a movie theater that had long since been shut down, but the building itself and its giant sign remained intact, defiant against its demise and seeming to promise that the show would go on, abandonment be damned. Marco only ever saw one film at the theater, some horror movie he could no longer recall, but he never forgot the building itself; the red carpet proudly laid out across both floors and across the stairway, the smell of tobacco from what Marco assumed was the owner's office, the giant oak desk near the entrance. Although Marco only saw the one movie, he had always enjoyed coming by as a child when his mother would force him to go downtown with her. He would disappear into The Majestic and be happy just walking around inside it. He always found it strangely fascinating and thought of it as a sort of oasis in a desert. The Majestic – like just about everything else downtown – was old to be sure, but there was something different about this lone structure. It wasn't merely old; it somehow felt vintage and unconquerable. Now, it was just another abandoned building, its doors barricaded and its windows boarded up. His thoughts lingered on The Majestic as he headed home. He would come across it shortly.

Through the swirling winds and the biting cold, Marco's thoughts were interrupted. He thought he heard something that wasn't the wind, indistinct and barely audible. He slowed his pace but kept walking. After a few seconds Marco decided it was only his imagination. He walked a little faster, but soon there it was again, just a little bit clearer. The sound hung in the air, delicate and enticing, but still undecipherable. He couldn't tell what it was, but the sound steadily felt like a siren's sweet and seductive call, and it felt like it was singing to him. *Come to me*, the sounds said without actually producing the words. Marco's heart began to race and for a moment he forgot the cold, forgot his desire to go home. He picked up his pace, completely fascinated, yet terrified of losing the faint, unknown siren's call to the windy night. The sounds grew steadily clearer and Marco knew that he was getting tantalizingly close to the source. That sound...THOSE sounds...I KNOW this.

Marco was a block away when he finally pinpointed the location of what had been calling him. It was coming from The Majestic. But it wasn't merely sounds. It was music! It was music and...just like that, he knew exactly what he was hearing. He heard the notes, six distinct cascading notes, melodic, haunting, beautiful. The six open notes were now mercifully unmuffled by the wind. The music pierced the night and for a moment Marco stood motionless in the windy, lonely night, amazed and suddenly overcome by the wonder of how he could be hearing what he was hearing.

Marco was now across the street from The Majestic, staring up at the barred second story windows that the music was coming out from. He stared, eyes wide. The music, the slow, looping six notes were coming from an electric guitar. That The Majestic had been shut down for over a decade and that electricity thus had no business working within those walls came as a vague second thought to the realization that Marco was hearing music from a song that he desperately loved at a time and place most unexpected. He remained motionless, unblinking and spellbound. For what seemed like an unfathomably long yet wonderful time, Marco stood outside The Majestic, leaning against the wall next to the front wooden doors, intoxicated and transfixed by music that seemed to invite him to become one with it, sing and dance with it. It was wonderful, like being lost in a magnificent reverie. The time of night no longer seemed to matter, the freezing wind no longer a concern. All there was in the world was this music, the unmistakable melodic notes reaching out to him like a lover's embrace. *It will be okay.* If a heart could simultaneously be scared yet healed of the same mark, Marco felt that the music was doing just that. He didn't question it nor did he fight it. He closed his eyes and tilted his head back against the wall, took a deep breath, and let himself be consumed by it.

He didn't know when the music stopped playing. So transfixed was he by the experience that he was unaware that the guitar had stopped singing to him. Subconsciously, that's what he decided the guitar was doing; singing to him. In Marco's head the music had kept playing, but the notes had ended minutes earlier. He opened his eyes. He wasn't sure how long he had been standing there. He looked at his cell phone. Just over ten minutes.

The night was quiet again save for the strong winds pushing against him. But he was no longer cold. He turned around to face The Majestic and tried to peek through the barricaded front doors. The thought belatedly came to him. *What...why was there anything coming from inside?* The building had been abandoned for years and surely any power would have been cut years ago as well. He leaned with both hands against the doors, trying to catch a glimpse of something – anything – inside. Nothing. He let out a sigh and let a foot come down heavily on a board that was lower down on the doors, just above the floor. The board creaked and gave way easily, falling to the ground with a clatter. Marco picked it up and looked at it for a second. The board wasn't nailed in at all. He looked just above where the board had fallen. The piece above wasn't nailed either. Only the top half of the wooden doors seemed to be properly boarded up. The bottom boards were left purposefully loose, set in place only by jamming the boards against the door frame. They could easily be pulled apart from inside or outside. Maybe so somebody could easily get inside in the middle of the night...?

Oh hell. Marco was just about to cover the doors back up and leave when he heard the guitar again. It was unmistakably a guitar, but this time the mysterious musician wasn't playing anything in particular. The guitar player just seemed to be playing random chords and riffs. But, again, Marco was drawn to it nonetheless. He bent down and reached behind the boards to where he figured the doorknob would be and fumbled blindly for it until his hand found it. He turned the doorknob...it opened. He backed away with a jolt and quickly turned around, fully expecting the cop he saw earlier to be right around the corner, gun drawn and ready to bust him for breaking and entering. But there was no one around. Then, without thinking or knowing why on earth he was doing it, he got on his belly and pushed the frail door open and crawled inside. He shut the door behind him and replaced the bottom boards as quickly and quietly as he could. It was almost pitch black inside. The only bit of light he could make out was almost directly above him. His memories told him that right in front of him was the staircase for the upstairs office and the lone screen room. He could see nothing on the floor he was on, but he remembered that it was a spacious room where there used to be arcade games and a concession stand where you could buy drinks and popcorn, as well as a small lobby if you just wanted to hang around and relax before the movie. His eyes slowly adjusted to the darkness and he could make things out a little better. The arcades, the concession stand, and the front desk with its fake plants remained where they had been years earlier, albeit under dusty plastic covers now. It was almost as if the owner just dropped everything one day and left, barely bothering to throw covers over anything of value before getting the hell out of dodge.

Sounds came again from upstairs and Marco held his breath. Shuffling noises and then a thump. A guitar again. But the person must have unplugged it. The music was now much more muted, but it wasn't an acoustic. Marco again saw the faint light above him. He went upstairs, slowly. *Oh man, I really am going to get killed by a homeless guy.* He was at the top of the staircase now, but the source of light faded and then was gone as soon as he got there. *Oh shit.* Marco felt a horrible sense of panic and he thought of running for the door downstairs, but decided against it. Whoever was here, if that person decided to chase after him, he would probably get run down before he got very far. His sight had adjusted as well as sight could adjust in almost complete blackness. He squinted and could just make out a figure in the shadows, just a few paces in front of him.

"Hello?" Marco managed to croak.

The figure in front of him immediately leapt to his feet and came rushing at him. "Whoa, wait!" was all Marco could say before the stranger tackled him. The impact almost sent Marco tumbling down the stairs, but he managed to twist his body enough to grab the railing, and he crashed to the floor on his back. Marco was trying to orient and defend himself, but the attacker was already on his feet, only a few steps away and brandishing the electric guitar in the air as a weapon. Marco was still on the floor, listening to his own short, panicked breathing as it echoed in the room.

"Hold on!" Marco finally said. "I'm sorry. I know I shouldn't be here." Marco tentatively began to get to his feet, his hands out in a nonthreatening manner. "Look, I'll get out of here now. Okay? You don't need to worry about me. I'll just go." The figure in front of him said nothing but kept the guitar held above his head. Upon closer inspection he saw that the person who had tackled him wasn't very big. In fact, he probably could have taken him down under the right circumstances. But this was definitely not the right time to try to prove how tough he was. He had no right to be there in the first place and there was no way for him to know if the person had a more substantial weapon than a guitar. But he knew he would rather not find out. Marco kept his hands up as he finally fully rose to his feet. "I'm going to get out of here, okay?" Marco said again. He was about to brace his hand on the banister to go downstairs when the person in the shadows at last spoke. "Wait."

Marco turned around slowly, stunned. He tried to put a face to the voice in the dark. It was a woman.

Marco stood at the top of the stairs, unable to say or do anything, shocked that a woman had managed to bring him to the ground and scare the hell out of him. He felt somewhat ashamed and silly about it. But he changed his thinking just as quickly. She could still try to hurt him and he wasn't really into fighting a woman, no matter the reason.

"Hold on a sec." the woman said. She moved away from him and reached into a large bag on the floor and pulled something from it; it was a lamp. She reached inside a jeans pocket and pulled out a small plastic object and the lamp came to life. The room glowed with a dim light, enough to distinguish what was inside the room but not quite bright enough to be seen from the outside. Marco could see the woman clearer now. She was wearing a black beanie to cover her short raven hair. She wore dark blue jeans and, like him, was also sporting a black leather jacket. She looked at him, her eyes sharp. "Why are you here?" she demanded, replacing her lighter in her pocket.

Marco wanted to ask her the same thing, but thought better of it. Instead, he said the truth. He heard music as he was walking outside and wanted to come closer to hear it better, that was all.

"Closer? You didn't come closer, you came inside."

"I know. I'm sorry about that." He looked around awkwardly. "I'll head out."

She ignored that last part. "So you heard music and decided to break in. Need I remind you of the laws against breaking and entering?" She didn't sound angry as she said it, but more matter-of-factly and almost amused.

"What, you did the same thing, didn't you? You just happened to do it first." Marco wasn't feeling so sorry anymore, but a little annoyed at being lectured about trespassing by a fellow trespasser.

"Fine," she said. She set the lamp down next to her and sat against a wooden beam, guitar on her lap. She started lazily strumming the guitar and seemed to forget anyone else was there at all. After a minute or so she looked up. "Yes? You're forgiven, okay? You can go. Just make sure you block the door once you leave and don't tell anyone you were ever in here." She nodded her head toward the staircase. "Bye." She returned to her instrument.

But Marco wasn't quite ready to go anymore. He tried to think of an excuse to stay a little longer, and decided small talk would be the best option to prolong his visit. "Why are you in here?" he asked. She stopped strumming the guitar and lifted it in the air as if to say *what does it look like I'm doing? Isn't it obvious*? But Marco just said, "Okay..." He looked about him and asked if he could sit down.

She studied him for a moment, probably wondering if he was dangerous, Marco thought. She must have decided that he wasn't. At length she said, "Sure." He moved closer to her and sat down, elbows on his knees, about three feet away. For a moment nothing was said. The girl went on playing her unplugged guitar as Marco sat next to her, watching her strum along, trying not to stare at her yet unable to do anything else. Even in the dim light he could tell that she was beautiful. She wore no makeup but Marco thought she didn't need any anyway. Her soft features and her fair skin glowed in the lamp light.

"I'm Marco. Marco Serra," he said. "What's your name?"

She looked up and eyed him quizzically again. She must have decided he was safe enough. "Alicia."

Marco got up clumsily to shake her hand and felt a little dorky doing so. "Nice to meet you," he said. Alicia looked at him a little amused and with a half-smile. She shook his hand. Marco sat back down but this time he sat a little closer to Alicia.

"So...why are you playing in here?" Marco said. "You could be playing that at home you know, where it's nice and warm." He felt confident enough to jest about Alicia playing in an actual home. This girl certainly didn't look homeless. She had an electric guitar for fuck's sake. And she was a little too well kept besides. And way too pretty. He refused to believe that such a beautiful girl could be without a home. But Alicia just smiled, as if she knew exactly what he was thinking. She chuckled quietly and then said, "Just need to get out once in a while. I come here sometimes to think and be alone. You're telling me you don't do that sometimes?"

Marco stared at her. "Well yeah, but I don't break into an abandoned building in the middle of the night to do so."

Alicia laughed softly. "Sweetie, you're here now aren't you? You're in no position to judge me." She smiled and looked straight at Marco's eyes. He felt his heart quicken.

"Besides," she said, "I'm not technically breaking in. Not really. My dad owned this building. I never knew what he planned to do with it after it closed. I think he'd actually forgotten he owned the damned thing. He still paid some random bill or another on this place even though he hadn't done anything with it in years. But eventually he just gave up on it." Alicia became quiet for a moment and stopped strumming the guitar altogether. A dark look came across her face, but she brushed it away almost as quickly as it came. "So you see, I have a right to be here. You on the other hand," she said with a smirk, her light coming back to her face a little.

"So why play in the dark then?"

"My dad didn't know I came here. No one did. This is like my sanctuary."

"The song you were playing," Marco said, "that's why I came here. I couldn't ignore it." He looked sheepish. "I know it doesn't really excuse me breaking in. It's just...I've always loved that song – you really have no idea – and well, what are the chances of randomly hearing that coming from an abandoned building at three in the morning?"

Alicia smiled at that and Marco found that he loved making her smile. Her smile made it impossible for him not to do the same. Marco was never particularly good at talking to women before, but for some reason he and Alicia were getting along just fine. Pretty extraordinary, he thought, given the circumstances of their meeting. More than anything he was simply glad for the chance encounter, even if the substantially self-conscious part of him was pretty sure he was only annoying her, and maybe she remained a little suspicious of him. But she showed no outward signs of it. And he didn't want to leave.

Alicia turned, guitar still in her hands. They were staring at each other now, studying each other's faces.

"This one?" Alicia's small hands went to the strings of her guitar. She played the first six notes of the song again, the same that drew Marco to this street, to this building, and to her. Marco's smile was all the confirmation she needed from him. She studied his face for a second, as if debating with herself, then smiled that smile again, though the slightest bit smaller now. Then she played the six melodic notes again, and she played the song from beginning to end. Again, Marco was helplessly captivated by the beautiful music and the equally beautiful girl playing it. He stared at Alicia as she played the song, beguiled by her effortless beauty and by the sensuous movement of her hands across the fret board. By now he made no pretense of not looking at her. His gaze remained on Alicia's eyes as she strummed, only briefly glancing down to her fingers as they played the strings of something more than her guitar. His heart was pounding. Alicia looked right back at Marco, and their gazes remained fixed on each other's eyes until the end of the song. When Alicia played the final note, Marco thought it seemed to echo throughout The Majestic, and he had the almost unquenchable hunger to lean over and kiss her. But he banished the absurd thought before he did something so stupid. *We've know each other for twenty minutes! She's more liable to punch me and not ever want to see me again.* Not to say that she actually would anyway. Still, he didn't want to screw up whatever chances he actually had.

They eyed each other for a second longer before Alicia broke the moment and turned to set her guitar down. Marco thought she looked just a little bit disappointed. But it was probably nothing more than supreme wishful thinking on his part. When Alicia checked her wristwatch, Marco instinctively reached for his phone to check the time as well. 3:57 AM. He had completely lost track of time, but he didn't care.

Alicia had gotten up and was now putting the guitar in its protective nylon cover. She was ready to leave. Marco didn't want her to go, but he didn't want to push his luck either. He stood as well, and waited. Alicia collected both her guitar and lamp and placed them in her large bag and walked to a metal footlocker in the corner of the room. She put the bag in the locker and was going back for the guitar amp, but Marco picked it up and carried it to the footlocker himself. She smiled and thanked him.

Whatever they had shared together only moments earlier was gone. They stood awkwardly facing each other, unsure what to say.

"I should go," Alicia said.

"Okay," Marco said, trying not to sound disappointed, and then they went downstairs. When they reached the front door they stopped again to face each other, ready to part ways. They peeked through the barricaded windows to see if anyone was outside before they broke back out of The Majestic. There was no one.

"You don't worry about being followed?" Marco asked. "I mean, what if someone wanted to try to hurt you or something? Or what if a cop sees you? I know your dad owns the building and all, but still."

"Owned," Alicia said, correcting him. "And I don't worry at all, at least not anymore. There's no need." She suddenly became very solemn. She squatted before the door and turned back to look at Marco. "I'll see ya then." She smiled, but it somehow seemed forced now. "Can I trust you to lock up before go?" she said, indicating the two boards at the bottom of the door.

"Of course," Marco said, a slow panic rising within him as Alicia started quietly removing the boards, ready to say goodbye for who knew how long. Maybe forever. She was about to crawl through the opening.

"Hey hold on," Marco said. Alicia got on one knee and turned once more to look at him. Marco squatted down to be at eye level with her, and when he did he became immediately self-conscious. His eyes gazing downward, now afraid to directly look at Alicia: "Could I...maybe get you number? Do you want to go out sometime?" When she didn't respond for several seconds, Marco finally met her eyes, trained directly on his own. From this distance Marco could now see Alicia's magnificently blue eyes. He felt as if he could see the ocean in them. He was consumed by those eyes, drowning in her powerful yet gentle gaze. He was lost in it.

"Are you sure?" Alicia asked. The question almost sounded like a challenge. "Marco..." Her face had taken on a completely different demeanor. She looked very pained and seemed to be reaching for something to say which she dare not mention. For the first time she seemed lost and almost at a panic, and looked as if she wanted to put voice to fleeting words that echoed aimlessly inside her mind. But either she could not find the words or she refused to speak them. Before Marco could say anything, Alicia recovered and steeled herself. Her countenance returned to what it was moments before. Her demeanor seemed slightly brighter, but her words did not.

"Some things are out of our hands, Marco," was all she said, even as she wrote on a small piece of paper and handed it to him. Her cell number, Marco thought. She buttoned up her jacket and adjusted her beanie and effortlessly crawled out the door and into the cold night.

As soon as Alicia was clear of the door, Marco quickly adjusted his own jacket to prepare for the weather before he crawled through the gap himself. When he was outside again, he pulled the old door shut and replaced the boards. He wanted to catch up to Alicia and have an excuse to talk to her some more and maybe even walk her home. He stood up outside, expecting to see Alicia either waiting for him or walking somewhere. He looked around him. The streets were completely deserted and – save for the wind – eerily quiet. There was nobody to be seen nor any footsteps to follow. Marco surveyed the area about him, disappointed and confused.

Alicia was gone.

Marco reached his apartment building several minutes later. On the way home he saw no one except the same patrol car from earlier in the evening. The cop did a great job of completely ignoring him again, but he couldn't care less. He walked past the main lobby and headed for the stairs to get to his second floor apartment. The apartment complex where he lived was built in the 1970's. It was nothing fancy but it was safe enough that not much security was required, clean enough that roaches and other bugs didn't wage a war to claim the place as their own. That was good enough for him.

Marco shut the apartment door behind him and threw his keys next to a carefully folded newspaper on the coffee table in front of the living room sofa. He plopped down on the sofa and put his feet on the coffee table, thinking about the past hour or so, still wondering what had driven him to go out in the middle of the night, but now satisfied with himself for doing so. He leaned his head back to the ceiling and closed his eyes and thought of Alicia. He looked back to the coffee table, to the folded newspaper. His eyes squinted in thought. But then he let out a tired sigh and tilted his head back once more, again looking to the ceiling, again his thoughts returning to the night and to Alicia. As sleep called to him and consciousness began to give way to exhaustion his reflections didn't waver. He couldn't really believe what had happened. These things didn't happen to people like him. Especially when it came to people like her. The last thing that went through his mind before falling asleep on his sofa was how much the night felt like such a wonderful reverie, how he couldn't have come up with something more perfect had he dreamed it.

8:30 that morning. Marco's eyes snapped open. The blaring of his phone alarm shocked him back to consciousness. He leaned forward and did a quick stretch, trying to shake the cobwebs off. Time to get ready for work. Marco got up and started heading for the shower. His apartment was a totally nondescript bachelor pad, relatively spartan and boring: a one bedroom apartment with a closet, kitchen and living room. Marco had no pets or plants or posters on the wall. His main sources of entertainment were the TV and his collection of DVDs, and an even larger library of books neatly displayed on a large black bookshelf next to the television. Besides that, his place had a very empty air to it, even for someone living alone.

As Marco was taking a shower he kept his mind on the night's events. He still couldn't believe it had happened. He remembered how his emotions had changed drastically throughout the night. How another night of nothingness metamorphosed into something exciting and terrific. Again he tried to figure out what had propelled him to do such a random and foolish thing as walking downtown in the middle of the night, almost asking for something bad to happen to him. At the same time, he thought how stupefyingly lucky he was for making that decision, and he congratulated himself just a little bit for it. It wasn't every day that that happened to him. It wasn't *any* day that that happened to him.

He stepped out of the shower and got dressed in his work uniform: blue jeans and a t-shirt. One great thing about his job was that he didn't need to dress up for it. It was very hands-on, blue-collar work and he liked it. He looked at himself in the mirror. He was taller than most people from his town and was fairly athletic. He had high cheekbones and light skin. His brown hair was kept short. He splashed water on his face and then went to the kitchen to prepare himself some breakfast. He sat at the kitchen table and saw the picture lying atop it: Marco with his parents. In the photo was Marco, standing between his mom and dad, his mom with an arm on his shoulder with a big proud smile; his dad showing only a grin but betraying as much pride as Marco's mother. Marco had no siblings. The photo was taken in front of Marco's high school at his graduation. Marco was never a great student. He loved to read and he had a fondness for the cable channels that talked about nature and history, but he never had much patience for school and in the seven years after high school he didn't get much more in the way of a formal education besides a few semesters in the local university.

In his teenage days, Marco and his parents worried that he wouldn't graduate high school. He remembered his mother talking to him earnestly on night, telling him to please take school more seriously – he was too smart to be failing. His father didn't say much, but when he did it was always something encouraging. He remembered how proud his parents had been that day, how much their faces beamed with unadulterated pride that their son was graduating – they never had a doubt. They always were encouraging him, and though they occasionally argued as any parents with a teenaged child would argue, he loved them and they loved him. Rose-colored memories as they may have since become, Marco remembered his parents – his only family – with tenacious love and the unavoidable feelings of loss and irreplaceability. Never again would he see his parents, and no new memories with them would be possible.

His parents were dead two weeks after his graduation.

Ruben and Cecilia Serra were killed by a drunk driver on an early Saturday night when they were returning home from one of their daily walks. They had almost made it. His parents were crossing a street two blocks from their house. The drunk driver, behind the wheel of a Ford F-350, turned a corner much too quickly and drove straight through his parents, never even slowing down. His father, absorbing the brunt of the impact, was killed instantly. His mother bravely hung on for several hours before succumbing to her massive injuries. Marco was on his way to the public library to sign up for the fall semester at college when he got the call from the police that his parents were in an accident. When he arrived at the hospital he was informed of his father's death, and that his mother was in the emergency room. Hours later, as he was sitting in a waiting room trying not to cry but failing to do so, a very solemn and exhausted-looking doctor told him that he and his medical staff had done everything they could to save his mother, but her injuries were too severe. She had died as well. Both of his parents were now dead, and he never got to say goodbye to either of them.

The following day, as his aunts and uncles (none lived in the same town) started showing up to grieve and to make preparations for the funeral, Marco saw the news coverage of the tragedy and for the first time got to see who was responsible for taking his parents from him. The man's name was Ramiro de la Cruz, a 47 year old unemployed drunkard who, during the trial, it became known that he would beat his wife when he would come home drunk, which, according to testimony from his wife, was fairly often. He was eventually sentenced to 18 years in prison and even though after the trial Marco never had to see the man again, he promised himself that he would hate him for the rest of his life. He would never forgive him. As it turned out, however, de la Cruz was murdered in prison by another inmate over a squabble about unpaid drugs. The other inmate stabbed de la Cruz twelve times with a melted down and sharpened toothbrush, leaving him bleeding to death in the prison showers. Marco had seriously considered sending the inmate an anonymous thank you note along with money for prison supplies, but eventually decided against it.

The day of the funeral, Marco made a point of avoiding his distant family and everyone else that showed up. He wanted to grieve alone and didn't want any of their pity or offers of condolences. He was never close to any of them and he didn't feel the need to change that now. After he buried his parents any connection he had with these people would be forever severed. His only close friend at the time was a school friend named Carlos Trujillo, a thin, dark-skinned metal-head with red hair. They remained amicable to the present, though the friendship was not nearly as close as it once was. Before the burial, Marco and Carlos hung out outside the funeral home, smoking cigarettes and doing their best to pretend that they weren't at a funeral. Carlos didn't say much, which was exactly what Marco wanted. Afterwards, the two bought beer and weed and went to Carlos's house. Again Carlos didn't say much and again Marco was grateful for the silence. That night Marco got shit-faced drunk and baked, and tried to forget that his parents were dead.

Marco had worn his jacket and started walking outside, but the weather had warmed considerably. He was about to throw the jacket back inside when he suddenly remembered the note Alicia had given him. He took it out from the jacket, stuffed it in his jeans pocket and walked to his beat up silver 1996 Ford Taurus.

During the drive to work, Marco thought about the note he had placed in his pocket, and kept patting at it to make sure it was still there, as if it would mysteriously disappear if he didn't keep close guard over it. But he refused to pull the note out, knowing full well that he would be tempted to call Alicia, and to be thinking about her all day. Not that he wouldn't be thinking about her anyway, but he didn't need the distraction – no matter how pleasant – from his responsibilities at work. At least that's what he was telling himself. Mainly he didn't want to appear desperate by calling Alicia so soon. Give her some time. He would force himself to avoid so much as checking what her number was until he clocked out...or at least until lunch.

Marco pulled into the parking lot fifteen minutes early. His boss, Benny Klonoa, was of course already there. He arrived thirty minutes early every day, both because he needed to open up Benny's Recycling Center, but also because, Marco suspected, he really did love his job that much. The recycling center was nestled about halfway down the eight mile road that led to the Boca Chica beach. One only had to take a small detour off the main road and you would come across it. It wasn't a huge center, and Marco liked the work because he got to be outside and drive around the city with Benny in his company truck and swap out recycling bins. It was actually kind of fun, and Benny was a good and entertaining man. Marco was also grateful for the fact that he didn't have to deal with customers all day long – a recycling yard is no Wal-Mart, after all – which was a good thing in his book.

Benny was in the office making coffee. When he saw Marco walk in he greeted him with his customary cheeriness: "Marco!" he said as he did every morning. Marco couldn't help but smile. He was amazed with Benny's perpetual brightness. The man was never in a bad mood it seemed.

"Morning, Benny," he responded in kind. Benny was a gentle giant of a Hawaiian man. He was in his mid forties, chubby and bald, and was the nicest man you could ever meet. Benny had offered Marco a job at the recycling center after running into him in front of Marco's apartment complex the year before. Benny had lost control of one of the large recycling bins as he was making his way down some steps and Marco stopped to help out. Benny appreciated the gesture, and after a brief conversation, Benny decided that he liked Marco and proceeded to offer him a job. Marco accepted and the two quickly developed a friendly employer/employee relationship. They got along splendidly.

"How's it going, Benny?"

"Pretty good, my man. I'm doing good." Benny definitely looked like it. He looked even happier than usual. "Hey, Marc, you remember Lisa right? The girl that was here a couple of weeks ago or so?"

Marco nodded. "Yeah of course." Lisa Cummings was a pretty woman Benny had met several months before, and the two were getting closer. Lisa had a younger sister that Benny had unfortunately never met, and now never would. Lisa's little sister had died three weeks prior, and Benny had been there for Lisa as a friend and as a shoulder to cry on. And maybe a little more. Marco didn't know how Lisa's sister had died and he didn't ask Benny. He figured it was none of his business unless Benny chose to tell him more about it. Marco made it a habit of not getting into other people's business unless he was completely sure that it was welcomed. He didn't even know the poor dead girl's name.

"Well, we went out last night," Benny said. "I wanted to cheer her up some since she was feeling down about her sister again. It's kind of up and down, you know? It's still so close since her sis' died, so when it does hit her it hits her hard." Marco nodded. "So we went out for seafood and then came back to my place and, well, you know." Benny had the biggest grin Marco had ever seen and he couldn't stop himself from grinning back. Benny deserved himself a good woman. He had lost his wife six years before to a brain aneurysm and he hadn't dated much since. Marco tried to encourage Benny to find a pretty and sweet woman again. A good man like Benny shouldn't be alone. Marco was happy that Benny and Lisa had found each other, and he had no doubt that the two were good for one another and that Benny would be nothing but respectful to Lisa during her grieving process.

"So how is she, Benny? Is she good to you? If she's not then I don't approve."

Benny laughed his big bear laugh and took a giant swig of his coffee. "She's a lot of fun, man. I mean, given the circumstances. We've been getting along great. I know we haven't known each other too long but, well, I don't know...I think things are getting pretty serious actually. But obviously right now I'm not trying to rush anything. I mean 'cause of her sister and all. But I think she'll be okay. At least I hope so. I've never lost a sibling so I don't exactly know what she's going through. I'm just trying to be there for her."

"Well good for you, Benny. I hope that Lisa feels better soon, and I hope things work out for the two of you."

"Thanks, man." Benny raised his coffee mug in the air in salute and gratitude. Marco returned the caffeinated salute.

"So how old is Lisa anyway?"

"Benny looked almost as if he was blushing but then he looked up with a sort of proud look on his face. "She's 34. I know what you're thinking. 'What's she doing with an old man like me, right?' I asked myself the same thing but hey I'm just gonna be happy she is."

Marco smiled. "Not bad. She's definitely a looker if you don't mind me saying." Benny laughed. "Well, you're a good man, Benny, so she must see that. And you've been there for her during this hard time so I'm sure she appreciates that. But damn, what are you, like ten years older than her? Lucky dog. Don't let her get away, Benny."

"I don't intend to!"

As Marco was enjoying the news that Benny was dating a cute woman a decade younger than Benny was, his thoughts returned to Alicia. How old was she? He hadn't even asked her but she had looked about his age, maybe a little younger. He would ask her when he called her later. He patted the note in his pocket again and moved it to his wallet instead. It would be safer there. Benny noticed Marco's change in demeanor and asked him what was up.

"Nothing," Marco said. But he was smiling and Benny picked up on it. It was a smile he recognized. A smile he probably had on his own face. He punched Marco in the arm and demanded to know what was going on. He had spilled the beans to Marco and he deserved the same, he pointed out. He was smiling as he said it, yet serious all the same.

Marco looked at Benny, who was now fully expecting to hear something juicy from him too. It was only fair. Marco told him how he was wandering around downtown for no reason, and that he ran into a beautiful girl down there. He was tactical in leaving out the part of him breaking into a building for this chance encounter. Marco said he ran into her on the sidewalk. Benny raised an eyebrow, but didn't question him too seriously. He was happier for Marco than he was suspicious about the details of his story.

Benny was now beside himself that the two of them had had such grand and simultaneous strokes of good luck. He lifted his cup of coffee in a second toast and Marco raised his own cup again as well. They chugged the rest of their now cooling coffee and went outside. It was time to begin the work day. Benny patted Marco on the back and pointed at him. "You tell me all about your new friend later today okay? Maybe we'll go for a beer after work!"

Marco said he looked forward to it and waved goodbye to Benny, who was off to a meeting with business people from the city. Marco was in charge until Benny came back. He snatched the keys for the forklift off the wall and as he headed for the forklift next to the giant cubes of crushed paper he started smiling at the idea of drinking with Benny. He had never drunk beer with Benny, but then again neither of them had had much to celebrate before. They certainly did now. Marco jumped in the forklift and the work day was under way. His day consisted – on the days that he didn't go out with Benny in his truck around the city – of organizing the large cubes of recycled paper and in grabbing the hundreds of plastic bags filled with shredded paper to throw in the bale machine, which would in turn churn out even more giant cubes of recycled and recyclable material. If he finished early he would take up janitorial duties and sweep and clean until the recycling center was as clean as a recycling center could reasonably be. Marco suspected that Benny didn't really need the extra help, but instead preferred the company. Marco appreciated it because he enjoyed Benny's company as well. Work didn't feel like work when Benny was your boss.

He did his rounds for the day, whistling and singing and in good spirits. Benny had found himself a good woman, and although he couldn't call Alicia his girl by any means, he couldn't help but think about her and smile. He looked forward to having a drink with Benny, and to giving Alicia a call. Come to think of it, he hadn't even told Benny what her name was. Well, there was always time for that when he and Benny went out for drinks. He remembered once more the song that brought her to him. So random, but he would take it. Life was good.

5:00 PM came around and it was time to clock out, but Benny hadn't returned. Marco thought it odd – Benny was never gone that long – but he didn't worry too much about it. Marco cleaned the bale machine, returned the cleaning supplies, and went to close the office. Benny had before given him instructions to close up the office and lock the main gate if it was time to close and he wasn't back yet. But Marco never before had to actually do so. *Guess I should go then*, he thought, a little disappointed that he may not get that drink with Benny after all, and wouldn't get to tell him all about his new friend. He unwillingly thought of the word girlfriend, and tried desperately to remove the thought from his brain. There were times that he had gotten way ahead of himself in that department, his mind subconsciously and prematurely latching on to a girl as being his girlfriend or lover and in those situations it always fizzled or downright backfired on him. *Well no shit*, the same mind said to him. He knew it was stupid and silly to feel that way about anyone, but he couldn't really help it. It was annoying as hell.

Marco waited another ten minutes to see if Benny would return, but he did not, so he left him a note saying sorry that he missed him and maybe some other time they could have that drink. He locked the office door and main gate from the outside, jumped in his car and drove back home. The paper in his wallet was burning and teasing him to open it, but he refused to acknowledge it until he returned home. He lit and smoked a cigarette to calm him down so he wasn't so jittery with anticipation about calling Alicia. He didn't want to make an ass of himself over the phone.

Marco closed his apartment door a little too enthusiastically and he thought that maybe he damaged the doorframe but he didn't care. His reservations about retrieving Alicia's phone number finally went out. He took his wallet out and the note folded inside it. He opened the note. As soon as he saw what was written on it, his face went from manic anticipation to complete disappointment and utter confusion. There wasn't any number written at all. What was instead written was something rather cryptic and not immediately meaningful. On the note there weren't seven digits, but words that appeared to be part of a book or maybe a poem. The note read: *Born to feel so close. Still I search. For you.* Below it was a postscript. *Look up again. Look up.*

The note trembled in Marco's hands and after several seconds he noticed that his hands were shaking. But his physical reaction to the note did not match the thoughts now swimming in his head. On the surface, Marco felt annoyed at what Alicia had scribbled. What the hell was that supposed to mean? The horrible thought that she was only messing with him flashed red in his mind. But Marco refused to believe that. That didn't feel right, didn't feel that that was the case. He knew that it may only be wishful thinking, but the shaking of his hands was not due to him being merely annoyed or disappointed. There was something else that Marco couldn't quite grasp, something that fluttered in his mind ready to be understood, but just as quickly disappearing as a morning mist colliding with the rising sun. Something about those words on that small piece of paper pounded in his head with unknown meaning, teasing him. But he couldn't figure it out. The words on the paper stirred and tantalized something within him, just as the song that Alicia played in the dead of night had done. But what? The answer felt so close, but the more Marco pondered it, the more it seemed to fade into a distant shadowy horizon.

"Fucking hell." Marco cursed the note, cursed Alicia's vagueness, cursed the silence of his apartment. He crumpled up the note and threw it on the coffee table and it landed next to the bundled newspaper. He sat down hard on the sofa and smoked another cigarette.

It had happened again. It had happened again and a damn fool he was for yet again daring to hope. He had dared to believe that a great night like the one before actually meant something, that it might, against all odds, lead somewhere. This time. But there had been plenty of other "this time's" and Marco had fallen for it – for them – every single time it seemed. What made him think that Alicia would be any different? *She never promised you anything you fool. It's your own damn fault for, yet again, getting way the hell ahead of yourself and acting surprised when nothing comes of it.* Yet...

He laid down on the sofa, confused and exasperated, the burning cigarette between his fingers close to his face. After a while of trying to clear his head he reached to the table for the discarded note. He opened it back up, reread it. *Born to feel so close. Still I search. For you...Look up again. Look up.*

Was that actually supposed to mean something to him? Why would Alicia even write something like that? Was that just her shtick or something? If she didn't want anything to do with him she could have just said so. She certainly wouldn't have been the first girl to do so. Marco had gotten used to the way women looked at someone when they meant to say "fuck off, fuck you" without actually having to say it. But Alicia hadn't looked at him that way at all. He didn't think so anyway. Marco read the note over and over until he felt like he was trying to memorize answers to a test. Hell, maybe he was. The note was vague as hell to be sure, but it wasn't dismissive of him. Alicia was probably just kind of a game or word problem freak, and this was some sort of benchmark Marco had to meet. Why bother writing anything at all if not to try to get something across to him?

At length, Marco decided that Alicia did mean to meet him again somewhere, somehow. However annoying or confusing the note had been, he would choose to trust that Alicia was sincere in whatever kind of bizarre detective games she was apparently into. He would play along and trust her. It would take a special kind of heartless woman to send him on a wild goose chase if she never wanted to really be found, though it was only a quick hop forward to conclude that there probably were special kinds of heartless people like that in the world.

But...not Alicia. Please not Alicia. He refused to believe it. Not her. Not this time. This time was different. She was different. She would not have let him sit with her, would not have talked with him, would not have given him any note to speak of, if she never wanted to see him again. She was trying to say something to him, trying to connect with him somehow. She wanted him to figure out her note and for Marco to go to her. He was as sure of that as much as he was sure that he had absolutely no way to prove it. But he knew. He had to believe that.

Marco looked to his right to the kitchen table, to the picture of him with his folks. For a while his eyes didn't waver from the figures of his parents, their faces so proud of him. He forced himself to look away from the picture, feeling a little ashamed. He was never comfortable with their unwavering pride for their only child. He felt like he underachieved and never really lived up to the amount of love his parents gave him.

Marco shook his head. *Enough! Enough with the pointless self-loathing. What is wrong with you*? He knew that he was being unfairly harsh on himself, but once the floodgates of ennui and guilt and depression burst open, it's not very easy to dam them back up. He looked again to the rolled newspaper, black and white, flush with the table. His thoughts wavered from Alicia to his dead parents. To Alicia. He reached for the newspaper, but pulled his arm back before touching it. He lay back and stared at it, and thought of Alicia and wondered if he would ever see her again.

-Six-

What are you doing? What are you thinking? Did you really believe such a thing as that, your happiness? That's so adorable! Yes you are so naive, so sweet. How many times do we have to keep coming back to this, love? Haven't you learned by now? What's it gonna take huh? When are you going to have enough of it? I mean, no offense – no offense there, sweetie, but I thought you'd have had enough by now. But you really are a sweetheart, I must admit, so the whole thing – your perpetual hoping! – the whole thing really is just so sweet. It's sad, of course! So very, very sad...yet I can't help but cheer your little-engine-that-could determination, even when you are flat on your face, bawling your eyes out. Oh don't think I don't notice that! Of course I do, love. I know everything about you, even if you don't, and it's all just so precious and I can't help but get swept away by it all: those big puppy-dog eyes you get when something good seems to be there – just for you! – and then that sad and desolate look you inevitably get when it all goes so, so wrong.

But that's what so interesting to me, darling! It's the cutest thing. I see through your eyes and I know how you feel. Oh I know that rush of adrenaline and excitement that courses through your veins once in a while – those moments that drag you out of your doldrums, out of your unimpressive existence. Oh believe me I understand! I mean who wouldn't understand, and who wouldn't feel as you do at those moments? Monotony and a life spent in the solitude of the background must be a bummer huh? Yeah I know, but don't give me that look now! It's not like you don't want this, you know. Remember you did ask for this. Yeah you know.

I know what you're thinking now. You're thinking to yourself that this is not exactly what you meant. You never liked giant masses of people – herds, you called them right? Oh how clever, darlin' – and all you ever asked for was a small group of people to relate to, and a good and pretty girl you could love and who would love you back. Oh! I am so sorry but I can't help but giggle when repeating that. You have been so wonderfully sweet to believe that, and so presumptuous to think that would actually happen to you! It's just all so cute. Yes, you believe that's not asking for much – but sweetie! – come on now, you know better than that. Don't be like that. These things you dream of aren't for you, so keep those hands out of the cookie jar! Your hands should never dream to reach inside that cookie jar of, let's just call it, the cookie jar of happiness. Why, you shouldn't even be in the same room! And you know this, baby. C'mon babe, let it go. Let it go, huh? You can't keep doing this to yourself. I say this 'cause I care. But one of us has to be realistic here, and I'm pretty sure it's you that needs to be so. Please, baby. Please?

We both know what's what. You shouldn't do this to yourself. It was cute, darlin', but it's not really cute anymore. C'mon, sweetie. Happiness? For you? Oh don't be silly! You're being silly, love.

Do I have to remind you? Come now, don't make me remind you, sweetie. Please, let us not go there. It won't be pleasant!

Marco's eyes snapped open and he stumbled violently out of the sofa. He was on his knees, holding on to the coffee table, shaking. Sweat dripped from his face and his breathing was ragged as he tried to collect himself. He tried to remember what the hell had happened and as soon as he recalled the dream he tried to shove it away just as quickly as it had come to him. He sat back on the edge of the sofa, hands on his sweat-drenched face, trying to control his shaking and fight back his own thoughts, hell-bent as they were in their masochistic mission of self-immolation.

When his breathing returned to normal he stood up and went to his bathroom sink to splash water on his face. He stood in front of the mirror, looking at himself, lost. The sweat on his face was replaced by tap water but he could not tell the difference. He hated the reflection staring back at him. His face betrayed no emotion but within Marco a thunderstorm heaved violently, threatening to drown him as if in an ocean, threatening to swallow him up and never let him go, all the while laughing at his pitiful attempts to escape from it. *You can never leave*, the voice beneath that ocean would say. You will not ever be out of this natural disaster that is your own mind. The voice that spoke to him as he slept whipped its final lashes at Marco before slowly receding into the distance and down into the depths where it came from. The voice had become braver, coming closer to shore, reaching its tendrils out to Marco, ready to wrap itself around him and pull him into the black depths of the sea. The dream and the voice had become more frequent. Marco didn't know how to fight it for much longer, or if he even wanted to. The voice in the dream had haunted Marco for years. At times he almost welcomed it. The thought of oblivion maybe wasn't so bad. Until recently he had only passively thought of being directly responsible for his own demise, but he wasn't fearful or necessarily in opposition to the possibility of it. He would never admit it to anyone, much less his parents. They wouldn't be able to handle that idea. But of course, they weren't around to say much of anything at all anymore. That last thought instantly made Marco feel guilty, but he couldn't help it. Every time he had the dream with the voice he was overcome with a sense of complete solitude and a pitiful fuck-the-world mentality. It was unoriginal and juvenile, but sometimes emotions got the upper hand on rationality.

Absently, he thought of the people who might miss him. Benny, probably. Benny was a great boss and Marco thought that they'd go out for that beer sometime after all. It would be a crime to leave Benny without having their drunken moment together. Carlos would maybe raise an eyebrow, but they hadn't been very close for some time. He'd probably drink a beer to Marco and move on, if that.

He next thought of Claire, and this made him laugh a little. Claire would probably get pissed off and call him a fucking idiot if he ever told her that breathing was becoming a bit of a hassle for him. She'd probably kick his ass if he tried. She'd be cursing him – probably out loud – at his wake if he actually succeeded. Marco smiled. Claire was something all right. She was unique. He was happy to know her, however strange their friendship was.

Marco thought of Alicia. His smile remained, but the smile was ambivalent. He was ecstatic to have met her, but Alicia had quickly become little more than an idea somehow, almost a dream. He knew he was being ridiculous and that it was neither fair to himself nor to her, but he needed something to reach and hope for. For so long Marco felt as if he was reaching out his hand in the darkness for someone who never reached back. He had no reason to expect Alicia's to be that hand, but he longed for it. He knew next to nothing about Alicia, but he knew that he wanted to know. That thought was clear to his very bones even if he couldn't explain it, and even though he was fully aware about how very stupid he was for already beginning to fall for someone he'd only met once and whom he knew almost nothing about. Marco didn't believe in the concept of love at first sight, and he would never put it that way anyway. But there was something about this that was eating away at him that couldn't easily be brushed aside.

Women, he thought wryly. But he knew that wasn't the problem. The problem wasn't women; the problem was Marco and his inability to make relationships last, his inability to stay with girlfriends he loved and – who at least said to him – loved him back. Yet they never stayed. His last relationship had failed two years ago along with much of his optimism.

Marco went to the refrigerator and got a Coors. Alcoholic company. He closed the refrigerator door and leaned against it, beer in hand. He thought maybe he should call Carlos to hang out, but changed his mind. He would have liked his company but he didn't feel much like chatting and catching up on things. That felt like obligated work and he wanted no part of it. Besides, he lived about an hour and a half away now. Marco doubted Carlos would want to come over in the middle of the week.

He thought of Claire, but he had even less hope of seeing her. Claire did everything on her own watch, and it was something Marco had found interesting about her when they first met, but had since become a bit of an annoyance. Marco had to learn to accept that she'd only see him when she felt like it, which could be at the most random if times. That bugged him sometimes, but she was too much of a fun and crazy person for him to forsake her friendship, even if it was lacking in time spent together. Maybe that was something that made it special. And when Marco and Claire spent time together they were almost always alone, which was just fine with him. Truth be told, Marco would have liked to have been more than friends with Claire. She was a potent mix of sweet and wild. She was short and petite, with nerdy glasses and a child-like love for anime, but she also burned rubber on her motorcycle and was fearlessly outspoken and certainly never boring. He would have loved to be with her, but he knew somehow that it just wouldn't work. He never brought it up and neither did she. Marco thought that Claire was likely with someone else, but he never asked and she didn't volunteer that information. A certain unspoken understanding was at play and Marco knew better than to push it.

Marco's thoughts returned to Benny and the beer that they wouldn't be drinking later that night. He would have to get Benny's number. Why did he not have it? They got along fine at work and they'd probably have a chance at being good friends outside of work. He wondered what Benny would say about the note Alicia had given him. He would probably just tell Benny that he hadn't called her and not get into what Alicia had actually written on the piece of paper. Benny had some news of his own after all. He would probably just ask Benny about Lisa and keep the focus on them.

Marco walked out of the kitchen and went to his living room to watch some TV before finding something to read. There was a commercial on about guitar discounts at some local music store. He regretted never having learned to play an instrument. Now would have been the perfect time for that. Maybe write some lyrics. Marco liked writing short stories but had never had the knack for writing lyrics. What good would they have been? It's not like he was going to have music to sing or play them to. He changed the channel on the tube. There was a show about learning how to survive in the wild (if you were that unfortunate bastard who managed to get himself lost in the arctic forest). He thought that surely there had to be some irony in becoming well-versed in wildlife survival, but having no clue how to adapt to a normal social life in his real world.

Just as Marco was about to learn how to trap a fat winter squirrel in a makeshift net and eat its raw, protein-rich brains, his phone began vibrating in his pocket. He pulled out the phone and checked who it was. Even if he had wanted to, he could not deny the smile that came across his face when he recognized the number. Maybe the night wouldn't be such a bad one.

"Hello?"

"Hey, you! Watcha doin?"

"Hey, Claire!"

"Hey you, what ya doing tonight? You busy?" Claire asked.

Like that, Marco's self-deprecating mood was shoved aside. Like other times before, Claire came out of nowhere to cheer him up with her sweet voice and not-so-sweet words. She could cuss like a drunken sailor on leave, and Marco loved it. Prissy women were not Marco's thing, and Claire would never be accused of being prissy. She'd kick your ass if she heard you say that about her.

"I had a shitty day at work and I need to get fucking drunk. You in, Marco?"

Of course he was in. He had never said no to her and wasn't going to now. Claire wasn't reliable when it came to availability, but she could definitely be relied upon for some good fun. He just hoped not to piss her off in the meantime.

"Yeah, hell yeah," Marco said. "I'm not doing anything right now. What do you want to do?"

"Duh. I just said get drunk, pendejo!" Claire Brooks wasn't very fluent in her understanding of the spanish language, but she picked up its vulgarity quite easily. She had, in fact, become quite taken to cussing people out in spanish. Marco was no exception, but it didn't really bother him. He actually found it kind of cute.

"I know, damn you," Marco said. "I mean, do you want to come over or go somewhere? I don't know how tired you are from work."

"Nah, fuck that, I don't want to deal with people right now. Stupid people calling in for stupid ass reasons. 'My cable isn't working.' 'Did you try restarting your cable box?' 'Oh no I guess not, silly me!' "Ugh, fucking people. Seriously. Read you damn manuals before you call to annoy me. Haha. Sorry, didn't mean to rant. But yeah I don't wanna deal with anyone right now. Let's go buy a case of beer and chill at your place. Is that cool?"

"Yeah come on over. I'll just clean up a little and we can go buy something when you get here."

"No don't worry about it. That's cool. I'll just pick up some Coors on the way and throw the beer in my backpack. You clean up your damn place. I want to get drunk as soon as possible."

That was indeed Claire, straight and to the point. Came and went like an ambivalent ghost guaranteeing that her haunts would prove not horrifying but a hell of a good time.

"Okay," Marco said. "I'll see you soon."

"Alrighty. Buhbye."

Marco hung up the phone and chugged the rest of his beer. It looked like the night wouldn't be a waste after all. He cleaned up and waited for Claire to arrive.

About a half hour later, the loud, insistent banging on the door announced Claire's arrival. Marco answered the door and there was Claire, case of Coors in hand and a tired but mischievous look on her face. She shoved the case of beer in Marco's stomach and after he set it on the table she gave him a big hug. "Been awhile huh? I missed you!"

"Yes it has," Marco said. "And whose fault is that?"

Claire gave him a look of acting hurt and laughed. "Oh you big baby. It hasn't been that long." She was still wearing her work uniform: khaki pants and a black work shirt with the logo of the company she worked for stitched on her breast pocket. Her long light brown hair was tied back in a pony tail. Marco thought she looked paler than usual. Her job dictated that she wouldn't get much in the way of sunlight, and like Marco, she stayed home more than she went out. She removed two beers from the case and said, "Let's put the rest in the fridge."

After packing the refrigerator with beer they went to the living room and sat on the floor like they always did. The sofa was usually ignored for some reason. It was cold in the apartment so Marco got up and went for a blanket and some pillows. When he returned he put on a horror movie on Netflix and lay on the floor next to Claire.

"So how was work?" Marco asked, aware of the response that would elicit and eagerly awaiting it. Claire gave him a look of annoyance and raised her beer in the air in a threatening manner, as if to throw it at Marco. But she had a smirk on her face and then laughed. Marco did the same and they both took sips of their beer.

"What about you, Marky?" Same shit different day?"

"Yeah pretty much, nothing really new. I was going to go out with my boss actually, but he didn't come back to the yard before my shift ended."

"Go out? You going to a strip club or somethin'? And you weren't going to take me?" She laughed and laid down completely flat on her back, beer resting on her flat belly, now exposed a little as her shirt lifted just a bit above her waist. Marco eyed her stomach for a second before looking up at her green eyes behind her glasses. Marco had no idea how she maintained her fit figure. She drank more than he did and never worked out. If he was a woman he thought that he would probably be jealous of her, but as it was, he was happy enough to enjoy the view.

"Um, no," he said. "But if I was going to a strip club I would definitely invite you. Though the girls would probably just be looking at you anyway. Not that I would mind."

She laughed again.

"No, me and Benny were just going to get some beer. He got a girlfriend and we were going to celebrate, you know, since he hadn't had a girl in awhile." He didn't mention the other half of what they were to celebrate. He didn't want to tell Claire about the weird note Alicia had given him; she would probably just give him shit. Besides, he still had the probably unreasonable hope in the back of his mind that he and Claire would one day have a chance. But he wouldn't dare say that either. If there was any hope at all, he didn't want to screw that up by bringing up some other girl. Not that Claire would be jealous. She didn't seem like the jealous type at all.

"Oh yeah," Claire said. "I think you had mentioned that before. Well good for him I guess."

Marco thought about Alicia and simultaneously pictured a jealous Claire and he absently smirked a little. Claire noticed the subtle change of expression on Marco's face. She stared at him until he looked back at her.

"...What?" Marco said.

Claire looked at him suspiciously. "Something on your mind, Marky? Someone?" She cocked her head a little. "Thinking about some other girl when I'm the one who's here?"

"What? No, no." He knew he was busted.

Claire's eyes widened and she smiled. "You are aren't you, you jerk!" She laughed and threw a pillow at him.

"No. I'm not thinking about a girl." He smacked the pillow over Claire's head playfully. He did his best to hide the lie. He had only just gotten the memory of Alicia out of his head when Claire called, but as soon as he mentioned Benny and his girl he couldn't help but be reminded of the night with Alicia, and what, if anything, he could do to see her again. It made him feel a little guilty about it since he was with Claire at the moment, but he couldn't pretend Alicia wasn't on his mind as well.

Marco adjusted the pillows on the floor and lay shoulder to shoulder next to Claire. They had become simultaneously close yet estranged since they met several months before at the local Barnes and Noble. They were both browsing the gothic horror section and started talking. Well, Claire had started talking to Marco would be the more accurate description. Marco saw her between the different shelf sections and was immediately attracted to her. But it was Claire who came up to him. She looked lovely even with the way she kept trying to cover her face with her hair. It was something he had always wanted to ask her about.

He was surprised how quickly the two had hit it off, and for a while it looked like their friendship might become something more. But it just didn't happen. For weeks this had annoyed Marco, both by the fact that their friendship didn't become something else, but also because it seemed clear that Claire never had a problem with that. But he learned to accept it, mostly. The first time that he and Claire got drunk and lay on the floor together, Marco had to fight the urge to kiss her. It was never overt, but every time they got wasted together and there was that moment of silently staring into each other's eyes, that with any other girl and at any other time signified it was time to take things to another level, Claire would break the moment by saying something funny or getting up to go for more beer or to go to the bathroom. And so it went, time after time, until Marco finally decided to give it up and accept friendship as the lone kind of relationship with Claire. It wasn't exactly bad anyway. Having Claire in his life was better than not having her at all, by far. Even if she wasn't there all the time it was still good.

The closeness between Marco and Claire at one time would have made him feel a little weird. The two lying shoulder to shoulder would have filled Marco with an anticipatory and frustrating feeling that he knew would not be satisfied. While that feeling and longing was definitely still there, he was mostly at ease with it. He no longer anticipated anything sexual with Claire, though it would have been a lie to say that he wouldn't welcome it. Maybe it was bound to happen that he would become completely okay with Claire's friendship and company without thinking about other possibilities with her. Or maybe it also had a little something to do with what happened the night before. The night that was so perfect, that despite the ambiguity of Alicia's note – and the even more ambiguous as to whether he would see her again – he was more hopeful about things than he had been in some time. Right then he decided that he would refuse to become disenchanted by the vagueness of the note, and to believe that Alicia did mean for him to find her. He promised himself that he would. He looked at the ceiling, beyond the ceiling, into the night sky, and sent himself back to the moment, alone together in The Majestic. Just the two of them and the music that had united them. He was smiling. He hadn't noticed Claire looking at him, who was now half-sitting up, resting on an elbow. She was eyeing him with a crooked smile and accusing eyes, somehow knowing quite well what he was thinking about, even though he denied it. She poked Marco hard in the ribs, breaking him out of his daydream. She laughed at him when he snapped out of it and reached for his side in pain.

"I knew it, fucker! I knew something fishy was going on here."

"What? What are you talking about?" Marco said.

"Uh-huh." Claire's green eyes were firmly fixed on him and she had a cute suspicious look as she studied Marco. The look on her face demanded answers without having to actually ask the questions. She didn't need to ask anything to get answers and she knew it. So did Marco.

Claire tilted her head a little and poked Marco in the ribs, harder this time. Marco squirmed a little and she laughed and poked him again.

"Ahh! Stop that!" Marco said, in pain but laughing nonetheless.

"I'm waiting," she said. She lifted her finger in the air again, threatening Marco. "I'll fucking poke the hell out of you until your ribs break, Marky. Tell me what's up. Come on, don't be a dick." Marco looked at her with a smirk to bug her just a bit more. It worked. Her eyes bugged up and she twisted her mouth in fake outrage and she poked Marco in the ribs again – this time with her middle knuckles – much harder than before. It was just short of a punch. Marco balled up, laughing and in pain, and rolled over to his side to avoid further punishment, at least to one side of his ribs. But Claire was merciless and followed him until she was over him, playfully poking and punching Marco until he finally gave in to her demands.

"Stop! Okay fine. Ah fuck I think you cracked my ribs goddammit."

They were both now on the floor, laughing and trying to catch their breath. Marco was in pain but amused and Claire stood over him again but gave him a short reprieve, laughing her ass off. She was ready to continue her form of enhanced interrogation if Marco still refused to talk.

"Speak! You don't want any more of this believe me."

Marco couldn't help but laugh again and said "Okay, okay!" when Claire flashed her unbearably cute Fake Outrage look at him again. "Alright, alright, chill out." But she hadn't budged. She was still over him, looking at him intently now, not how she was only seconds ago. She was no longer laughing or even really smiling. She was staring at his eyes, as if judging something. She had never looked at Marco in quite that way. But in the split second just before it became uncomfortable, her smirk returned and she sat back down, close to him. She was more serious now, but her smile had returned a little. Marco got up, rubbing his ribs as he did so. Claire laughed again, quietly this time. Marco gave her a sidelong glance and grinned. Her smile widened and Marco was happy for it.

Then Claire's smile got smaller. "So, tell me about her," she said.

9

Claire went home a couple of hours later. She asked how Marco had met Alicia, and as he had told Benny, he told Claire that they met when they were both walking around downtown. He wasn't comfortable telling anyone about how he had really met Alicia. One reason was because he knew that people would think it weird and maybe a little creepy. But the other reason was that he wanted to keep of the meeting between Alicia and him secret. It was their little place, just for them. A sanctuary, Alicia had called it. And so it was becoming for him as well. He felt a little guilty about not telling Benny or Claire the full truth, but he thought it didn't really matter anyway. The point was that he had met an attractive and sweet and interesting girl. That's all that should matter. The case of beer was nowhere near finished and would have to be saved for another day. After Marco finished talking about Alicia, Claire said she had to go home. It was rare that they didn't kill their beer completely. Claire said that she had to leave, got her keys and went for the door. Marco followed her to the entrance to say goodnight and when he did, Claire had turned around and gave him another hug, longer than any before. She looked up at Marco and slowly, lightly, kissed him on the cheek. Marco was surprised but didn't step back, just smiled. Claire looked at him a few seconds longer then jabbed him in his sore ribs again. When she saw Marco laugh she said goodnight and turned around to go down the stairs to her bike. Marco waited until she was out of sight before closing the door. He was feeling pretty good now. He had had a good time with Claire even if she had probably cracked a rib or two, he thought, lightly rubbing his side again. He downed the beer in his hand that was now getting warm. He thought of Alicia and began wondering how he could get a hold of her again. He was happy that he and Claire were becoming closer but he wondered if telling her about Alicia had been a good idea after all. She had seemed okay with it but he didn't want her to feel like he was ditching her. Claire had been good to him, a good presence in his life. When she was around anyway.

Marco brushed his teeth and went to lie down on his bed. Claire had to understand. They weren't together. Of course she knew that. But you never really knew with these things. He was starting to feel guilty about it and he wasn't sure why exactly. She had kissed him on the cheek, and she had never done that before. Maybe it was no big deal. He'd just have to ask her about it later. He closed his eyes and thought of the night before.

-Ten-

Marco. Marco? Hi, sweetie. Oh, Marco. What did I tell you? Oh, I told you then as I've told you so many times before, but you never do listen do you, hon'? Why don't you listen to me, sweetheart? You're only hurting yourself. But you don't listen to me. I only mean to protect you, don't you see? Oh, I'm so sorry, baby. I am truly sorry but you need to learn. You need to learn because you really need to grow out of this and let it go! Let it go. The sooner the better. The sooner you can give up your silly notion of being happy the sooner you can, well, go back to just being! This is what it is all about for you anyway, darling! You know this. But here you're making me do this to you. This could all be so simple for you. So simple. Just believe me. No? You refuse to believe me. Oh sweetheart. I'm so sorry. Then you'll just have to remember. I'll make you, Marco. I'll make you remember them. I know you don't want to, honey. This will hurt and you will cry and cry all over again. You will cry and be sad. But that's what happens when you try to find that elusive happiness, Marco. Don't you think there's probably a good reason why it eludes you, why it continues to evade you, day after day, year after year? Oh poor Marco! I can see you getting that sad puppy-dog face already. Are your eyes burning yet, Marco? Do you feel your face drooping just a bit? Are you feeling that urge to stare at the ground, to cover your face in shame? Well it's not like anyone cares, silly. But I'm wondering. Just wondering. And this is your last chance, Marco. This is it, and then you'll have to remember, remember the sadness and loneliness you experienced for wanting more than what you deserved. Be honest with yourself. You really should know your place. Just accept it. Will you accept it? No? Okay then...sweetie. Okay. I tried, babe, I really did.

Do you remember that girl? Oh what was her name, what was it...Oh yes! Angela! Ooh she really was pretty. Yes she was quite the looker. Do you remember how you used to sit behind her in class, how you used to think she had the most beautiful skin you had ever seen? The sensuous shape of her neck, the silky smoothness of it that you just wanted to reach out and touch with your fingers. Oh I know the way you looked at her when she went to class wearing those form-fitting blue jeans and her hair up in a bun. It drove you wild huh Marco? Oh yes it did. Don't be bashful now. Remember, I know you, love, better than you could understand. Remember how when you decided to finally ask her out – do you remember what happened, sweetie? You went up to her and asked her out, just like that! Oh the sheer hope in your eyes that day...But sadly, Marco, sadly, we know what happened next don't we?

She laughed at you, Marco. She laughed! Why, she didn't even have the decency to say anything! She only laughed at you. She laughed and then turned and walked away. And baby, that wasn't the end of it, was it? You still had to see her every day at school, and then she told all her friends and they all laughed and talked about you as if you weren't even there. Then you hated her so! You wanted her to disappear forever for being so heartless.

And what of Nadia? She was something too. You didn't even hesitate with her. Anyone would have been so proud of you. You were like a little trooper. You just went after her. You saw her working at the music store and you weren't about to let her get away were you! You saw that cutie in those black Tina Fey glasses and that beautiful smile and you knew you needed to talk to her. Oh Babycakes, you were so valiant in your effort to get to know her. You thought you would hit it off and I have to give you credit – for a while you actually did! You, of all people actually had a chance. Or so you thought. Right, baby? 'Cause then what happened? Out of the blue, she tells you she's getting back with her ex, and she says she can't see you anymore. Like that, at the snap of a finger she dropped you like a sack of rotten potatoes. You were no good to her. You were no longer of any use. You were a placeholder. Poof! She was gone. But of course she was, darling. Of course she was. Of course they all will be. Once and for all, please drop this. Because this isn't even the tip of the iceberg is it, love? This isn't the regret and hurt you experienced at other times in your life. Do I have to bring them up too? Do I, darling? Please don't make me. It will only make you sadder. All you need to do to avoid the sadness is to just give in and accept, Marco. Give up this foolish dream of lasting joy. Give up and just be. It will make things easier for you.

And what of your parents? Your parents, Marco. Think of them. Imagine their disappointment about what you've become. That photo of you and them. How proud they are of you. But what should they be proud of, Marco? How have you rewarded their pride? All their support, sweetheart. All their kind words and thoughts about you. But look at you, sweetie. What would they say about you now? What

*would your parents think about their good son now? Shall I
elaborate, Marco?*

11

Marco woke up with a start, his heartbeat racing and a shimmer of sweat growing on his forehead. He wiped the sweat from his face and sat on the edge of his bed, annoyed at having his good night ruined by the same damn recurring dream. He asked himself why he was having the dreams with the voice more often, but inside he knew why. And he could not deny the truth coming from the voice. The voice was simply subconsciously reiterating what he sometimes felt when he was awake and thinking about Claire or Alicia or any other girl that he once cared or had hopes for. Or his place in life and how his parents would have felt about him now. His dead parents. But he didn't want the thoughts or the voice constantly in his head. He didn't need a reminder of his life's failures. He had gone through them already. He had had the dreams with the voice before, but never this often. Why were they working overtime now?

He rummaged through his messy nightstand and found a pack of unopened cigarettes. He pulled one out, lit it and went to the living room. He stood in front of the window and opened the blinds. He looked at the trees outside, their branches swaying with the wind. He touched the window glass and it was cold on his fingers. This night, just like the previous one, was a very unseasonably cold and windy one. But the day had been as warm as any other South Texas day, which was odd. That was more of a California kind of day.

"Damn bipolar weather," Marco said. "Make up your mind."

He opened the window and immediately felt the blowing winds rush into his apartment. Outside, the trees shook and the wind howled, as if trying to frighten the mostly empty city streets and force its residents back into their sheltering homes. Other than the wind it was eerily quiet, even for night. Marco finished the rest of his cigarette and flicked it outside. The wind quickly picked it up and carried it across the sky to the west. *Damn. Look at that cig go!* The heavy winds had tossed the cigarette high in the air and the cig was making its featherweight journey in the direction of the Mexico border. *Maybe it's an illegal immigrant making a break for it back across the border, dodging the authorities. Go ciggy go.* He smiled, amused at how easily an airborne cigarette had relaxed him and, momentarily at least, made him forget the dream. He peeked out of the window and looked toward the direction the now long gone cigarette had flown to. If he twisted his head he could almost make out the border stations where the border patrol and city police guarded the bridge that led to Mexico. Marco never went to Mexico anymore. The only times that he used to go over there were when his parents invited him, and even then only a few times. His parents used to go across to Mexico at least a dozen times a year. Medicine and food were much less expensive and they enjoyed visiting friends, and if only in a limited and symbolic way, they liked to honor the place where they were born. Marco never felt truly connected to his Mexican roots and he felt a little guilty about it. His parents were proud of their heritage. Marco felt neither pride nor shame. He just didn't feel any personal attachment to it. The concept was as foreign to him as it would have been if someone had told him that he was the descendent of Irish immigrants. He missed his parents terribly. He missed them more than he would admit to anyone. He was terrified that admitting it aloud to another person or even to himself would be too much to take. He wished he had spent more time with his parents. He wished he had told him he loved them more. He didn't do that enough, not nearly enough. His mom was the sweetest person in the world. Cecilia Serra would talk with anyone and cheer that person up if he or she was feeling blue. She would shelter a wounded animal if it came crying and scratching at the front door. Marco remembered when he brought home a homeless cat, half dead from malnutrition. His mother saw the pleading look on Marco's and the cat's eyes and said, "Go get a bowl with milk. Who knows when the poor thing last ate anything." Marco didn't know if it was the pitiful look on the cat's face or his own that warmed his mother's heart. Probably both.

His father Ruben was a strong man who did his best to raise Marco to be self-sufficient. His father was a self-taught man who was determined and stubborn enough to start his own lumber business. Marco had worked under his father for several weeks and was starting to learn the ropes. His father's hope was to teach Marco enough about the business to one day leave it in the charge of his only son. But that day would never come. Soon after Marco started working for his father, both of his parents would be dead, viciously killed by a man who couldn't dream to be half the person that his parents were. They were taken from him by that sorry piece of shit. Marco was left alone. His parents were gone and the business went under. Marco had no idea how to run his father's lumber business.

He worked random jobs until he met Benny. He took the job at the recycling center because he thought Benny was a decent guy and that the job actually sounded kind of fun. He also took the job in large part because it reminded him of his father, and the business that he once ran. He thought that maybe, in some small way, he would redeem himself by at least being a small but useful cog in someone else's successful business. But he didn't really believe he could ever fully make up for his shortcomings as a son. He would have to live with that. And rose-colored glasses or not, there wasn't anyone that would convince him to think of his parents as anything but decent and loving, and gone much too soon.

Marco looked back to the border to where his cigarette had vanished. Mexico. Maybe he would go visit his parent's place of birth again someday. They would probably like that. They had encouraged Marco to take pride in his heritage and were disappointed when Marco refused to join them. *Stupid. What would that have cost you?*

To the left was the University of Texas at Brownsville, the city college just across the street from the border crossing. Many students would come from Matamoros and other Mexican towns to attend classes. When Marco attended classes and the professors asked where students were from, chances were high that a good percentage of students were from Mexico. Not that that was anything to complain about. A lot of beautiful girls were from the other side of the border. He thought about the classes he had taken and some of his professors. He had always preferred the night classes. He liked the emptiness of the campus when the sun went down below the horizon and few students roamed the college grounds. He had especially liked professor King's Literature class that he had Monday nights. The man was a genius and hilariously offensive. If Bill Maher had been a college professor instead of a professional comedian surely that's how he would have been. King's class was challenging and fun. Marco remembered one night when he was leaving class. He had been jazzed by a uniquely lively lecture and was outside the classroom and starting his walk back to his car. He had gotten his iPod from his backpack and hit shuffle as he usually did Monday nights after Lit class. He remembered the strange sense of wonder he had felt as he walked the campus walkway and looked up at the giant clock tower to the far west of campus. He looked up to the clock tower and to the night sky, just as his favorite song began to play. A rapturous feeling of bliss overcame him as he looked at the gorgeous, glowing campus lights, as he looked up to the sky, and as the hauntingly beautiful six note introduction to his favorite song was underway...

Marco flung himself away from the window, his breath escaping as if someone had just punched him in the gut. That night after his class, as the song began playing he had looked up at the night sky. *Look up.* Alicia, that's what she had said. *Born to feel so close. Still I search. For you. Look up again. Look up.* He looked in the direction of the university in disbelief. No way. There was just no way. It couldn't mean the same thing. How could Alicia possibly mean the same thing? He had never told anyone about that night. There was no way anybody could know, much less someone he had only met for roughly half an hour. He had never uttered a word about it, he was sure of it.

Marco lit another cigarette and stepped outside of his apartment building, standing in the mostly empty parking lot, his gaze set dead center in the direction of the university. There was just no way. Alicia had to have meant something else by what she wrote. She had to. This made no sense. Marco located his car and sat on the hood, his confused vision still firmly fixed on the college grounds. Outside it was cold and windy and he was shaking again, but it wasn't, Marco knew, because of the chilly weather. He stared and tried in vain to convince himself that what he was thinking was ludicrous and foolish. What he had felt that night years ago as he was leaving class, and what Alicia had told him were impossible to reconcile. They couldn't be connected. But what else could Alicia have meant? Marco could come up with no other explanation, crazy as it was. Nothing else would have made any sense to him. Not that this explanation did either, but it was the only thing that he could come up with.

Marco jumped off his car and walked to the end of the parking lot, just before the lot turned into the city street, resigning himself to the possibility that the explanation that made the least amount of sense was also the one that made the most sense. But how?

Alicia? Do you want me to find you there, at the school? Look up again, like that night? But...how in the world could you know, Alicia? The cold wind pushed against him, harder and more insistent than it had before. The temperature felt as if it was dropping by the minute. Marco could see his breath appearing and dissipating in the air as he breathed in and out. The swirling wind got even stronger and shoved Marco forward a couple of steps onto the street – a couple of steps closer to the university – and Marco felt and instant sense of fear at what he could not deny. Whatever it was, it wanted him to go to the place where his vision was unwaveringly fixed upon. Marco knew exactly what he was feeling again. It wasn't just realizing that Alicia's note and his experience that night were somehow connected. It was the exact same thing he had felt the night before, the sense of having something call to him, demanding his attention and presence. The same voice calling him, and the same sense of helplessness, knowing that he couldn't deny the voice. Like the night before, he knew that he wouldn't say no. He couldn't. He would go to the university and see Alicia, or whatever it was that was beckoning to him now. He tried to relax his breathing and tried not to dread who or what he might encounter.

   Turning back to his apartment, Marco tried to calm his nerves and tell himself that the last time this happened it wasn't a horrible thing. He had met Alicia. Whatever had happened the night before was a good thing. Maybe this would be good as well. The thought seemed to help. By the time he climbed the stairs to his apartment the shaking had at least subsided. He threw on his jacket, got his keys and locked the door behind him. He would not walk this time. It might be Alicia again he sees or it may be someone else or no one at all, but if he needed to make a quick getaway from whatever may come after him, then he wouldn't be completely unprepared or with no way of escaping. When he got inside his car, he took a deep breath and started the ignition, and began the short drive to his former university.

12

Marco parked his Taurus in a residential neighborhood just outside the campus grounds. The neighborhood was dead quiet as Marco walked past the old wooden houses that bordered the school. The campus had been built over and around people's century old homes about fifteen years before. Since there wasn't enough land available to build the school, many residents were offered compensation to move away so that construction could begin. Most took the money and moved away without incident but a few old-timers with deep-rooted attachments to their homes had initially refused to leave. But those who had houses in the way of the would-be university eventually all did move, even if only a few blocks from their original locations. They probably had no real choice in the matter.

The walk to where Marco imagined he was supposed to be would take about seven minutes. He had made the trek to this particular part of UTB plenty of times and had memorized the time it took. He took out his iPod. The thought came to him that if he was going to somehow try to recreate or relive – or whatever the hell he was supposed to be doing – the event that happened to him years before then he should listen to the same song he was listening to when it happened. And to look up. Everything felt about the same. The weather was cold and windy like the night before. He turned up the volume on his iPod. When the song played, Marco was immediately brought back to what he felt that night. The same sense of mystery and, somehow, of peace. He remembered the clock tower, the university lights, the night sky. He was back exactly where he was those years prior, living out that night again. And then he was no longer wary about what might happen. The moment was again...just right. At this time he needed nothing more. The campus lights and the star lights and the school and the sky melted into one beautiful, luminous sphere. Marco fell into the cosmos and swam in its magnificence. He was home. His eyes watered and his cheeks moistened. He cherished the bliss all over again.

A bright flash of white light in the distance brought Marco back. Of course. University police. Of course they were patrolling, they did so twenty-four hours a day. How could he forget? Marco wiped his face with his jacket and collected himself. It would be a complete waste if he came here only to get busted by security for trespassing. He would just have to try and hide from their sight until he figured out what exactly he had to do. Being discovered and subsequently questioned by the fuzz would mean nothing but bad news. How was he supposed to explain what he was doing there if he himself didn't have a clue? *Well sir, you see, I've been having these weird thoughts in my head these last couple of days, and now I'm looking for some girl who gave me this cryptic not, see? I don't even know if she's here or not, but I really, really need to find out, you understand me? So if you'd be so kind as to let me wander around campus for a while, I'd sure appreciate it. Thanks*! Yes, for his honesty he would probably be rewarded with a trip to one of Brownsville's finest steel and concrete hotels. And maybe even earn himself an appointment with a friendly person wearing a white coat, comfortable sofa and medication at the ready. He wasn't so sure he didn't need it. He wasn't too optimistic about convincing others about his motives to be at the school. It was best to avoid that scenario entirely. He ducked into a dark area between two buildings and waited for the light to pass. The guard went by without suspecting anything. As soon as Marco was sure the guard was far enough away and he was in the clear, he jumped back out from between the buildings but kept to the shadows as best he could. If he was going to find Alicia he needed to do so quickly. If he was going to find *anything* then he'd better move quickly. He continued along the white cement walkway past an intersecting street in the direction of the clock tower and where his Literature class had been. If he was going to discover anyone or anything then it would presumably be somewhere in that area.

The plants and trees seemed just as they were last time Marco was here. Even the armies of cats that had taken up residence and claimed dominion over the campus years ago were ever present. What before had seemed like a small band of felines was now a thriving society of peaceful, lazy cats, effortlessly asserting their ownership of the land. The cats roaming the grass or clambering up trees always made him smile, and they did so now.

Marco was just about to reach the building where he had professor King's class and he felt a tinge of anxiousness building inside him because nothing was happening – nobody was around. Even security was nowhere to be seen or heard anymore. The thought occurred to him that even if this is what Alicia had meant – he was at least somewhat sure of that – it didn't necessarily mean that she would be there now. She could have meant for Marco to be there at noon tomorrow, or at three in the afternoon six months from now. She could have meant not in this damn place or anywhere near it. She could have meant nothing more than she was just messing with him. But he didn't really think that to be likely. He had no way to know that of course.

Marco saw a fat, gray cat then running through the grass at full speed. Probably hunting something, he thought. His gaze followed the cat as it pounced off the grass onto a tall oak tree. When the cat reached the top of the tree and after Marco followed it for a short while, he stopped walking and stood frozen to the spot. He was looking up at the clock tower. He didn't see anyone or anything, but he knew. Just like last night. He didn't hear music and he didn't see Alicia but he didn't need to. He felt his heart thumping quicker, anxious at the anticipation of what was to come. Where are you, Alicia? If it's really you again, where are you? He turned and looked around in every direction, ready to spot her between the buildings or sitting patiently on a bench somewhere. But he could not see her. Then, out of the corner of his eye he saw a figure, barely visible. He squinted and he saw the figure look at him for a brief moment, just long enough for him to confirm who it was. Alicia. She was standing about a football field away. As soon as he recognized her he smiled radiantly. Even at this distance he knew she was smiling back. But just as she did, she quickly turned away and walked toward and behind the college bookstore. Marco, suddenly panicked about losing sight of Alicia, took off running after her, mindful of the loud clapping noise his shoes were making on the cement in the otherwise silent night. The figure of Alicia – as well as his smile – grew larger as he got closer to her. He caught up to her as she was making her way to the end of the large building. He slowed to a fast walk when he was a dozen paces away from her.

"Alicia," he said. But she kept walking without turning around. They were now next to the old wooden buildings that used to be the campus police department. They were now boarded up and abandoned, the police having since been relocated to another section of the campus. In front of Alicia and adjacent to the old police buildings was one of the streets that ran through and around the entire university. Alicia crossed the street without looking to see if anyone was around or if there were any cars coming from either direction. Marco knew that the chances of anybody driving by at this time were slim to none, but it still annoyed him and made him hold his breath when Alicia crossed the street so casually. When he saw that she made it across safely he kept walking after her.

"Hey wait up," he said again. But again she ignored him and kept walking. She was now on one of the many large grass fields on campus. The fields were frequently used by students – and cats – when they simply wanted to relax. This particular area was about a football field in length and width and led to the lake at the center of the university. At the end of the field there was a long wooden pier that stretched about a quarter of the way to the other side of campus. At the edge of the pier there was a small white house with a round bench inside where students could sit and look out at the lake and the surrounding campus buildings. In front of the little house at the end of the pier was a little space where you could sit and dangle your feet over the water. Marco figured Alicia was heading there. She was. The field itself was at a decline so it wouldn't be easy to be spotted by anyone not standing at the top of the field and staring directly at their location. It wasn't particularly well lit either.

Marco caught up to Alicia and walked with her side-by-side to the pier. "Hey," he said. She didn't say anything, but she glanced at Marco and flashed him a small, mischievous, half-smile and kept walking. Marco was content with that so he shut up and they walked to the pier in silence.

When their feet hit the wooden boards of the pier Alicia finally broke the silence. "Surprised, Marco?" When he could only manage a blank stare she laughed quietly under her breath. They reached the end of the pier and sat inside the round little house close together, their legs lightly brushing against each other. Alicia didn't slide away to get extra space, and Marco made no attempt to do so either. He had no idea what to say to her. He was ecstatic to see her but was still in shock that she really was there, his hunch miraculously proven true. They were sitting with their backs to the field, facing the lake. Alicia said nothing, her eyes fixed upon the water, as if lost to it. Marco could think of nothing to say regardless, so they sat in silence, enjoying the sight of the water swaying back and forth in the ever-windy, cold weather.

Marco felt his teeth start to chatter and zipped up his jacket. He turned to Alicia and saw for the first time that she didn't have any real protection against the weather at all. She was wearing blue jeans and a dark green shirt with a band logo on it. Her tennis shoes were dangling off the end of the wooden bench, she was so short. Marco felt guilty for not noticing that Alicia wasn't wearing warm clothes and for not offering his jacket to her earlier. He took it off and offered it to her.

"I'm sorry. It's really cold. I should have offered it to you earlier. Here you go." He raised the jacket in front of Alicia and right away felt the near freezing wind against his skin.

Alicia turned to him and said, "No thank you. I'm not cold at all, really. You keep it."

"What? You've got to be kidding me. I was cold *with* the jacket. You must be a popsicle right now. Take it. I'll feel like a jerk if I'm the one wearing it."

"No, don't worry about it. You're the one that's cold. I can hear your teeth rattling." She gave Marco the sweetest smile that almost warmed him enough to not need the jacket. Almost. "You're sweet. But no you keep it. I'm not cold. Don't worry, okay? I really don't need it." She laughed very quietly, barely audible. "Honestly I wasn't cold last night either. I think I'd just covered up out of habit. But I'm not cold. You keep it, okay sweetie? And you're not allowed to feel bad about it." She did her adorable smile again.

"Are you sure?"

"Yes."

"...Really?"

Alicia gave Marco a look of mock annoyance and put her fists on her hips. Then she grabbed his jacket out of his hands and threw it at his head, laughing. "Put it on will you?"

"Alright, fine. But you can't make me not feel bad about it." He buttoned up the jacket and covered his head with the hoodie. Alicia had nothing covering her short, straight, raven hair. She looked absolutely gorgeous with her unbound hair blowing in the wind, the ends of her dark hair caressing the light skin on her lovely face. Marco wished the ends of her hair were his own fingers. He wanted to touch her beautiful face. Her neck, when the wind blew her hair just right, gave Marco an even greater longing for her. She had a small and slender figure and she was beautiful.

"The water is gorgeous isn't it?" she said.

"Beautiful," he said, not looking at the water. Alicia turned her vision from the lake to look at Marco when he said this. She dipped her chin a little and looked up at him. Her blue eyes were as dazzling as the night sky and the shimmering water beneath it. Hypnotic. Marco was consumed by her eyes, and he had to force himself to look away before he said or did something he might regret.

"So," he said, shifting in his seat and trying to regain a semblance of composure. But nothing came out of his mouth. He wanted to ask her about the note, about how she could have known what Marco had experienced that night, alone, and about what she was doing there. He had so many questions about how it was possible they were both at the same place, at the same time, yet again. But his mouth seemed incapable of bringing those words and questions to light. As strong as his need was to find out what was going on – there was a stronger voice now preventing him from doing so. A warning in his mind collided against his desire to know, imploring him not to pursue that path. Don't do it, it said. You don't want to do that. You don't –

"Tell me about yourself, Marco. Tell me about you. This is the second time we meet like this. Let's assume there won't be a third and this was our last time talking. What would you tell me?"

Marco was taken aback by what she said. He didn't want to hear anything about not seeing her again. He felt sadness at the possibility and wanted none of it, especially now.

"What do you want to know?" He was afraid of boring or disappointing Alicia by telling her about his life. What was there to tell? His parents were dead. He had an okay but not particularly well-paying job. He had a spectacularly mediocre life, how 'bout you?

"Oh don't be like that. Come on. Everyone has a story to tell. Everyone has skeletons in their closet, if that's what you're worried about. I would know."

"You tell me first then, about you," Marco said.

"Ha, nice try but I did ask you first. Obey the rules." She reached her hand out, her eyes directly on his, and rubbed a soft hand on his arm for encouragement. It worked.

He let out a long, quiet sigh. "Alright. Well, I used to come to school here. I was here for a few semesters but I dropped out. I don't know. It just didn't feel right. Felt like I was wasting my time I guess. I've been working at a recycling center for a while now. It's an okay job. I don't hate it I mean. It's kind of fun actually. My boss is nice. You'd like him I think." He didn't tell her that he had already brought her up to him.

"Okay. That doesn't seem so bad, Marco. College isn't for everyone. Plenty of artists and musicians never went. At least you gave it a shot, and that doesn't mean you can't go back sometime in the future. And you don't hate your job. Not everyone can say that. So what else? Family?"

Marco put his elbows on his thighs. He really didn't want to talk about his parents.

"What's wrong?" she asked.

"I'm an only child. I grew up here with my parents."

"Okay. Go on."

"They're dead. They were killed by a drunk driver a couple of weeks after I graduated high school. The guy driving took a corner too quickly and hit my parents as they were crossing the street. My dad died right there but my mom managed to hold on a little longer. She died in surgery. I didn't get a chance to say goodbye to either of them, no final words like in the movies. They both were just gone."

"I'm so sorry." Alicia reached over to Marco and hugged him, her face resting against his neck. He felt wetness on his cheek and he realized that Alicia was crying. What the temperature hadn't managed to do to Alicia his story had. She was gently shivering against him. Marco wrapped his arms around her and hugged her back. Her warmth and her breathing against his chest felt good. He wished it were under different circumstances, but holding Alicia was as perfect as he had imagined. But now it was Marco who was uttering words of comfort to her. "It's okay, Alicia. It was a long time ago."

But Alicia continued to shiver under his arms. She said something so quietly that Marco could barely make it out.

"What was that?"

"I said that it's not fair." She sat back a little, but her arms remained around his neck, and his stayed around her waist. Her eyes were puffy from crying. Marco wiped away her tears. Alicia smiled, but not with her eyes. He thought that there was something else troubling her, something that she wasn't telling him. He waited for her to continue.

"The death of a loved one." She suddenly seemed a million miles away.

"What's wrong? What is it?"

"You don't know. I want to tell you but I don't know how." Her eyes were wide. "It's out of our hands."

Out of our hands. It was what she had said when they first met, as she was leaving The Majestic. What was she talking about?

"What's out of our hands, Alicia? What can't you tell me?"

She shook her head, hopelessly. "It's out of *my* hands, Marco. Out of *my* hands. I don't know why or how it's happening, but you need to know on your own. You may already. You just need to accept it. I just..."

"Accept what? What are you saying?"

Alicia only shook her head. She pressed her cheek against Marco's hand and hugged him, harder. "I need to go," she said, and got up and started walking back across the pier to the field. Marco quickly stood and went walking after her.

As they were crossing the field, Alicia silently reached a hand for Marco's and their fingers wrapped around each other. She covered both their hands with her free hand and leaned into him as they walked, shielding her small frame. She said nothing. Whatever was going on, Alicia knew, but she wouldn't – or couldn't – say what it was. He wondered if it was the same thing that was preventing him from asking Alicia about the information that only he should have been aware about. When the thought occurred to him, he knew that somehow it was so. And just as it had before, the words he wanted to say remained firmly locked in his mind. He also didn't want to further upset Alicia, so he didn't fight for the words he wanted to say.

Before reaching the end of the field and stepping onto concrete again, Alicia stopped Marco. She looked at him solemnly. "Marco, listen to me. You need to be strong here and not give in. Do it for yourself. And...do it for me. You will remember, I promise. And you must be strong. I wish I could tell you but I can't. And I'm so sorry. If you can't do it for you then do it for me. Please." She stood on her toes and kissed Marco on the cheek, the same cheek that Claire had kissed.

Marco just looked at Alicia, not knowing what to say or how to feel. He was about to protest that he didn't know what she was talking about, but the look on Alicia's face would not let him.

"Okay," was all he said. "Okay."

They crossed the street back to the campus walkways without talking. When they reached the area where the clock tower looked over the university and where Marco had his night class, he remembered about security. He hadn't bothered to keep an eye out. His thoughts had been only on Alicia and in trying to decipher what was going on, and trying to make sense of what she had said. As if on cue, a white light appeared in the distance to his left. The light, at first unfocused, suddenly pointed in their direction.

They were spotted. The light grew larger and larger. Alicia jerked Marco's hand and turned him almost violently to her. Her eyes were watering again, the blueness of them reflecting brightly in the campus and star lights. Before he could think to say anything, Alicia grabbed him by the collar, pulled him down toward her, and kissed his lips. He returned the kiss, his arms encircling her small waist.

Then Alicia tore away from him and was running down the walkway and behind the old police department. Marco turned to see how close the security light was now – *very* close. Shit! He turned back to Alicia. She was at least thirty feet away from him now. He froze for half a second before running after her. Alicia was already running behind the old buildings. Somehow, he knew what to expect by the time he got there, even as he refused to believe it. When he turned the corner of the buildings, he came to a dead stop, breathing hard. He turned and punched the building's rotting wood as hard as he could, ignoring the pain in his knuckles. He stared at the space behind the buildings where Alicia should have been, but there was no one.

13

Claire opened the door to her house and shut it behind her. She rented an old white house with her best friend, Dana. The two had made a pact after high school to leave home as soon as possible. It wasn't that they had such terrible childhoods or adolescent years at home; they were simply desperate for independence, whatever the cost. Their longing to get out of the houses they grew up in come hell or high water had led to this: two women working relatively low-paying jobs that afforded them enough wiggle room to pay the bills, food, and of course, the booze. Claire walked inside quietly, careful not to wake Dana. She always got pissy when you woke her from her slumber, like an angry lion whose tail you just stepped on. Dana Smith had long blonde hair. She was much taller than Claire – taller than Marco even – but Claire and Dana were very similar otherwise. Like Claire, Dana wasn't going to win many people over with her blunt and fiery personality. Together the two had come to an unspoken agreement that they would be nice to people once, and if that didn't work – if they were insulted or mistreated in any which way – well then the jerks knew where to go and Claire and Dana would be more than happy to give them proper directions if they didn't, likely with knuckles to their chins. Claire and Dana met in high school and had become thick as thieves almost immediately. They were both essentially loners. Most of either of their "friends" were guys with nothing in common with them, who wanted little more than to sleep with Claire and Dana. Claire and Dana occasionally obliged. The caveat was that Claire and Dana always took charge of the who, when, where. After Claire and Dana became inseparably close, the men were removed from the equation almost altogether, at least for the remainder of their high school years. Claire and Dana became exclusive lovers for the next few years and neither of them missed the men they had been with. They had meant little to begin with. Now they were the best of friends and were still occasional lovers.

Their house was a two bedroom home with barely-working plumbing and peeling beige wallpaper. The house creaked and it was too cold in the winter and way too hot in the summer. They loved it. It was theirs, their home, no matter how shabby it looked or was. It was their baby. The house and the bills were paid out of their own pockets and they took care of the old thing. They took pride in trying to scrub this lump of coal until it shined like diamonds, even though it never really did. They knew it was a silly endeavor but they didn't care. It was home.

Claire walked in the dark, trying not to bump into things as she made her way to her room. She squinted her eyes toward the living room as they adjusted themselves to the darkness. Dana had fallen asleep on the couch again. She liked to stay up late watching movies. The TV was still on but Claire didn't turn it off. It would probably wake up Dana. Claire found the remote and slowly lowered the volume to zero and then went to the small closet in the hall and got a blanket for Dana. She carefully draped it over Dana, kissed her on the forehead, and retreated to her room. She shut the door and threw herself on her bed without turning on a light. She looked up at her ceiling and then out of her window, saw as the dark was disturbed by the occasional passing vehicle in the neighborhood streets.

The night at Marco's had not gone as she had wanted. She had expected and was looking forward to getting drunk and hanging out with him all night. It had been a while since she had seen him and she missed him. She had told him as much, but she never allowed him to know how much. She couldn't. That would make her too vulnerable. She told Marco she missed him the same way she would tell anyone else. It was disingenuous, but she couldn't bring herself to open up to him and tell him so. She tried not to admit it even to herself.

Claire looked out her window and thought about the day she met Marco. She had been so angry. She had gotten in a terrible argument with her ex-boyfriend in the mall parking lot before they had even stepped out of his stupid Mustang. Dave was yelling and accusing Claire of cheating on him. Dave was red in the face and calling her a bitch and calling her a whore. He was implacable. When Claire had had enough of his nonsense she told him so and made to get out of the car. Dave grabbed her hand and yanked her back inside and told her to shut the fucking door. She jerked her hand away and asked him what the hell his problem was. Dave had never gotten physically violent with her. His accusations, while becoming more frequent, had never been anything more than disrespectful yelling. Claire thought that Dave would never cross the next unspoken line. She was wrong. When she dared to talk back to Dave and as she turned around once more to step out of the vehicle, he grabbed her shoulder and forced her around to face him. He balled his fist and punched her under her chin. She got immediately, wildly pissed off and punched Dave right back, right to his nose, almost breaking it. Dave's eyes went crazy and he grabbed her by the hair, trying to knock her out and punch her into submission. Claire managed to turn her face just enough to avoid taking the impact but his fist connected with her ear. Bright white light and nausea swam across Claire's vision for several seconds, completely disorienting her. She was beyond fuming but she couldn't tell up from down or Dave from car door and this pissed her off even more.

Before she could think of anything else to do or say she stumbled out of the car and slammed the door in Dave's face, crushing the fingers on his right hand as they reached out to grab her. She held on to the roof of the Mustang and tried to orient herself. Her ear was stinging and ringing loudly. She flipped Dave off through the window and rushed to the mall, alone. Dave was howling in pain at his badly crushed fingers and he called Claire a bitch again and sped off, driving with one hand and holding the other in front of his face in agony and disbelief. Claire hoped that she had severely broken the bastard's fingers.

Claire made her way inside the mall, shocked and furious. Nobody had ever hit her. NOBODY. She had told herself many years earlier that she would never allow anyone to lay hands on her like that, and if anyone ever tried then she would make them pay dearly. She hadn't done that. The best she had managed to do was flip him off and punch him once. She was angry that the bastard's nose hadn't broken. She wanted to see blood running from Dave's face, ruining the precious interior of his beloved Mustang. She wanted him to bleed to death inside his own car. She was beyond angry with Dave but even more so with herself. She had let herself down.

"Motherfucking son of a bitch."

She was fuming by the time she walked inside the women's bathroom to inspect her face. She looked herself in the mirror and saw the left side of her face and chin. Her chin ached like a bastard but she couldn't see any marks. It would probably just be unbelievably sore for the next several days. She lightly touched her ear and it stung like a thousand wasps. It was candy apple red from her ear to the middle of her cheek. A middle-aged woman came out of one of the stalls and stood in front of the mirror next to her. She stared with wide eyes at Claire's red face and murderous expression.

"I fell." Claire said without emotion. *Fuck off. This is none of your business, lady.* The woman left without a word, obviously worried but compliant and clearly frightened of Claire.

Claire went inside one of the bathroom stalls, lowered the lid and sat on the toilet. She folded her knees to her arms and willed herself to calm down. She was not going to cry. She refused to cry on account of that scum. He would not have that power over her. He would not...

She cried. She felt her eyes burning with the need for release and she could no longer contain the dam. The levees broke and tears flowed down her cheeks in streams. Her face contorted in anger and she punched the concrete wall hard, scraping her knuckles and tearing the skin. She looked at her red knuckles and punched the wall again, and again, until her hand was bloody and throbbing and shaking. After a few minutes the shaking and the crying stopped but she was angrier than she had been at any point in her life. How could she let him do that do her? She shook her head and dried the last of her tears.

Cheating on him. The bastard had some nerve. Cheating on him? He was the jerk showing up late at her house drunk off his ass and wanting nothing more than a drunk, sloppy lay. He was the one who insulted her and showed up late or not at all. He was the one who had cheated on her. He had slept with a coworker and she only found out because another female coworker of his had told her. Dave hadn't even tried to deny it. And she forgave him. For some goddamn reason she had chosen to forgive him and now he had the gall to question her about her own fidelity?

Fuck that. She should have cheated on him. She should have cheated on him and more. She should have slept with his best friend, taped it and had it mailed to Dave in a black heart-shaped box. She had every right, especially after what had just happened. She hadn't officially dumped him and she would find a way to get back at him. She would find the first decent-looking guy and seduce and sleep with him and tell Dave about it before she told him to fuck off forever. She would give that guy what she hadn't given Dave in a long time. She was incredibly glad she hadn't given herself to Dave in weeks. It was becoming a chore anyway, not anything remotely pleasurable. Now she would sleep with someone else and enjoy every single meaningless moment about it. That would royally piss Dave off. Good. It would quite officially end their god-awful relationship and she would get herself off in the process. Two birds one stone.

Claire left the restroom. Shoppers were going about their business. She hoped no one would come up to her. She got to the center of the mall and stood there for a second before deciding to go to Barnes and Noble. Bookstores had a way of relaxing her. At the very least they would help her get her head straight. She continued walking and touched the left side of her face. It was tender and would probably bruise horribly. It was a miracle her glasses hadn't broken as well. She flipped her long hair forward across the left side of her face to cover her cheek and ear. No need for inquisitive or pitying eyes.

When she walked in the bookstore she allowed her mind to sort of numb out what had just happened to her. The memory of the last few minutes temporarily faded into the background. She was already becoming lost in other thoughts as she started browsing through the books. Nothing terribly interesting in hardcover. She was about to set the book in her hands down and head over to her favorite section – gothic horror – when she saw Marco. He was in her gothic horror section casually browsing through a novel. He was wearing ripped jeans and a Joy Division t-shirt. Claire stopped for a second, considering. *He's cute. He'll do just fine.* She forced herself to become detached. She absently picked up a random book and leaned against a shelf, the book in her hands dangling lazily over the side. She bought time to see if he would look at her. He did. Several times. She felt some pride in that. She walked over to him and pretended to be interested in another random book she pulled from the shelf.

"Hey," she said to the stranger.

Her new acquaintance – probably about her age, she thought – looked up from the book he was using as a cover to pretend he wasn't looking at her, and smiled.

"Hey...What's up?"

He was adorable. Claire couldn't help smiling in kind. They talked in the store for half an hour and Claire found herself actually liking the guy – Marco he said his name was. She was annoyed at herself for finding him likeable. She didn't want to like him. She just wanted to use him and forget about him. He was supposed to be a weapon against Dave, a fun but meaningless lay. She couldn't find him interesting. She mustn't give a damn about him.

But she did. He was so goddamn sweet to her.

Eventually they left the store and went their separate ways. Claire had given Marco her phone number when they were leaving the mall, but as she walked away to call Dana to come pick her up, Claire began to second guess her motives for giving Marco her number. She remembered Dave and felt the rage returning. *Yeah. That's why. He's just for sex. Don't start caring.*

That's what she told herself the first few weeks when they would hang out together. He's nothing more than a lay. But every time they were alone and she knew that she could have easily seduced him, she always held back. After a while it became moot. She knew she couldn't do that to him. She had really started to like him and she couldn't just sleep with him and forget him. And she didn't want Marco to think she was just a conniving bitch if she told him the truth, if she told him why she began talking to him in the first place. If Marco had tried making a move on her she would not have hesitated to give herself to him. But he was so goddamn respectful! Or maybe just afraid of being rejected, she didn't really know. There had developed an understanding between them that she didn't fully comprehend. She was frustrated. She liked Marco and wanted him, but she was afraid. She felt that if she made the first move then she would be forced to be honest with him, and she was terrified of losing him because of it. He wouldn't forgive her for trying to use him and then discarding him like nothing. She had lied to herself about her reasons to see Marco, but as the weeks and then months passed he had become a good friend. He was becoming more than that.

That night, however, her mind was not yet in the right place and she had no way to know what Marco would begin to mean to her. She was bitter about what Dave had done and her aching and bruising face would not let her forget anytime soon. When Dana arrived to pick her up and she saw Claire's suspicious new hairstyle she pulled the car over and demanded to see her face. There was no way she could keep it from her. Dana's eyes narrowed dangerously and only said, "Dave" as she looked at Claire. It wasn't a question.

Claire nodded. Dana held Claire's hand all the way home and neither said anything until they arrived. Then all hell broke loose.

"I fucking told you I never liked him! I never trusted him. How could he do this to you? I swear to god I'll kill him! If I ever see him again I will beat his ass. Claire, you need to press charges against him."

Claire said nothing. She was sitting at the kitchen table, listening to Dana vent and trying not to cry. Dana cooled down and went to her. She hugged Claire to her, gently touching Claire's bruised face and brushing her hair with her fingertips.

"I'm sorry, sweetheart. I'm sorry. I just don't want anything to happen to you. I never want to see you hurt like this. It's not your fault."

Claire didn't want to hear anymore, and she didn't want to talk. She just wanted to clear her mind and relieve her anxiety and stress. Her anger. Her head was resting on Dana's breasts as Dana was brushing her hair with her fingers. She put her hand on Dana's stomach and slowly turned to look up at her. She lifted Dana's shirt and rolled her fingers over her bare skin as she moved her mouth slowly over Dana's shirt, over her breasts. The fingers caressing Claire's head froze and Dana was looking down at her, her eyes questioning but not rejecting Claire's mouth and fingers.

You sure? Dana's eyes asked her.

Claire nodded.

Dana took Claire's hand and they went to Dana's room. They made love that night and it was exactly what Claire had needed. Dana was extra sweet to Claire and was cautious about not hurting her bruised and swelling face and Claire loved her friend more than ever. But after she and Dana had finished making love, what was on her mind was not revenge against Dave, and it was not her love and appreciation for her friend who would be there for her until the end of time, and it was not her battered face. It was all of those and none at once, because what was at the forefront of her thoughts was the image of a sweet guy that she hoped she would not begin to care for.

14

Claire was woken up the following morning by the sound of the stereo in the living room. Dana liked to wake herself up in the morning by blasting Nine Inch Nails across their entire house. Claire liked their music too but she wished her friend would psych herself up in the morning a little more quietly, like with an iPod. At least she knew what to buy Dana for Christmas now. They both worked at the same call center, and while neither would ever say that they enjoyed their work, Dana took great sadistic pleasure in relishing her work role of sarcastic bitch. Hardly a customer ever hung up without an indelible memory of Dana Smith. Claire never understood how her friend managed to keep her job. Their employer was probably just afraid of Dana. Or in love with her. Either way, Dana took full advantage of her long leash. She was fearless.

Claire rolled herself out of bed and went to the bathroom to wash her face. Even with the bathroom door closed behind her, she could still hear Trent Reznor shrieking his lungs out across the house. She washed her face and brushed her teeth and grabbed a towel from the above cupboard. She sat down on the edge of the tub holding the towel in front of her face. Already she was thinking of Marco. His face flashed in her mind but she was unable to make sense of it. There wasn't anything she could do was there? Would it be right for her to try anything? He had already found...he met someone. She shook her head, trying to will Marco out of her morning thoughts. *It's your own fault. What did you honestly expect?*

The smell of bacon and eggs and the sounds of clattering pots and pans in the kitchen brought her back. Dana was cooking breakfast, bless her heart. Claire left the bathroom and went to the kitchen. When she walked into the kitchen Dana gave her a mischievous look and pursed her lips at her in a kissing motion. "Good morning, sexy," Dana said.

Claire smiled at her. She liked to sleep in nothing but bra and panties and when Dana saw her like that in the morning she always commented about it. She was sweet to her. Dana always slept in baggy pajamas so Claire couldn't exactly compliment Dana's lovely figure in those shapeless pajamas that wouldn't make anyone look sexy.

"Mornin', babe. Food smells good!"

"Yeah of course. Who is doing the cooking here? One of us had to provide us with delicious food. It sure as hell ain't you."

Claire gave Dana a lazy, just-woke-up smile. Dana noticed right away that something was bugging her but she said nothing. She scooped up the eggs and bacon from the frying pan and put them on a plate. She served herself a plate as well and carried both of them over to the kitchen table and set both down in front of Claire. Claire looked puzzled. "Trying to fatten me up?"

Dana raised an eyebrow at Claire and gave her a *missy, don't you worry your sweet little heart about it* look. She came back with two glasses of orange juice and put them next to the plates. She grabbed a chair from the other side of the table and sat right next to Claire, wrapping an arm around her and giving her a hug and a kiss on her temple. She patted Claire's leg from underneath the table.

"Now, we're going to enjoy our breakfast," Dana said, "and when we finish you are going to tell me what's wrong. This is not up for debate."

Claire opened her mouth to speak, and then closed it. She really hated her friend sometimes. She couldn't keep anything from Dana. She was a goddamn mind reader. About a decade of close friendship had to have its disadvantages as well she supposed. But Claire knew that that wasn't fair. She knew Dana just as well as Dana knew her. Claire gave Dana her best look of faux anger and said, "Fine." She began stabbing at her eggs with her fork.

Dana stuck her tongue out at her and Claire laughed, almost spitting out her half-chewed breakfast. Her bogus demeanor was undermined by her friend's silliness. She loved her.

"Good girl," Dana said, patting Claire on her bare thigh again. "Let's eat."

After breakfast they got dressed extra early so they could talk. They sat on a creaky old bench in front of their house. The sun was bright and hot, even this early in the morning. Dana was waiting patiently. She wasn't going to let Claire off the hook. She would call in sick for both of them for the next week before that happened. Dana had a good idea what was on her mind, but she wanted her friend to say it. Claire was twiddling her fingers, buying time. She hooked a loose strand of light brown hair behind her ear and turned to Dana. She had a faint smile.

"It happened," she said quietly. "I waited too long. He met someone. And he seems happy about it. I just waited too long, you know?" Her eyes were big and moist.

Dana knew who she was talking about of course. They had talked about Marco many times. Claire had told her that she thought she was falling for him, but that she couldn't tell him. She couldn't tell him that she originally only meant to use him; that she kept telling herself that he didn't mean a thing to her; that he was a tool to be used up and discarded. He had been too good to her. She didn't know when she actually started to give a damn about him. But she did now. And it terrified her. Dana had encouraged her to just come out and be honest with him already. Claire knew that she was probably right, but she couldn't do it. Now it seemed too late.

"What exactly happened?" Dana said.

"He said he met someone. A pretty girl." She shrugged. "Said they met downtown or something."

"Downtown? Since when does he go there?"

"Actually this is the first time he's ever mentioned going there. I remember him telling me he hates it. Anyway, what does it matter? He found someone, probably better. Wish him the best. Gotta move on right?" She pulled out a Camel and lit it.

"You know you don't mean that."

"Sure I do."

"Come on, Claire. Who are you trying to fool?"

"Well what the hell am I supposed to do? I met him dishonestly and I kept lying to him for my own selfish reasons, to use him. And now that he meets someone new and I guess I feel left behind – now I choose to be honest with him? I'm just being selfish all over again. He wouldn't trust me and I wouldn't expect him to."

"Sweetie. Claire, you're being way too hard on yourself. Did you ever tell him about what happened with Dave? That same night you two met?"

"No." She thought it over a second. "Why?"

"Well, from what you've told me about him he seems to be an understanding person. Just tell him what happened with that jerk. Let him know how you felt then and how you feel now and that there is a world of difference between the two."

Claire crushed her cigarette against the bench and flicked it at the front porch. "But that's just it. I don't want to tell him. I don't know, I just can't."

"That's another thing there, Claire. If you want to tell him how you feel then do it. But you can't keep this to yourself and expect him to just hang around and wait for you until you're good and ready. You have to choose."

Claire let out a frustrated sigh and laughed. "I know. Yeah I know."

"So what will you do?"

"I have no idea. Cry. Hunt that girl down." She laughed. "Maybe I should just accept that I fucked up and that I have to live with it now. Maybe I should just keep it to myself and keep being friends."

"It's up to you, babe," Dana said. "But what I would do is take the plunge and tell him. Whatever happens then it happens. And I'm here for you."

"I know." Claire smiled. "Thank you." They hugged.

Dana checked her phone. It was time to head out to work. "Okay! Time to go piss off some annoying callers. Whatta ya say?" They jumped into their green Neon, their shared work vehicle, Dana blasting heavy metal music all the way.

15

"Valley Cable, we appreciate your call, my name is Dana, how may I help you? Yes. Yes ma'am. Of course I can help with that, I love helping my customers." The unnaturally high pitched way she said it did nothing to mask the sarcasm in Dana's voice. Claire, sitting away from Dana in another cubicle, did her best to suppress a laugh and failed. Dana was her daily dose of antidepressants at work. It was a slow day and she had no one on her line. She rested an elbow on her chair and put a hand on her chin, amusedly watching Dana be Dana. "I am so sorry to hear that, Mrs. Kowalski..." Dana was over exaggeratingly pretending to hang on to her caller's every word, doing her most simultaneously sweet and condescending voice. "Okay, ma'am, can you please try unplugging you cable box and resetting..."

Dana stuck her tongue out at Claire and put her fingers against her head in the shape of a gun and shot herself. Claire laughed again and got up to take a mini-break. It wasn't like her phone was lighting up with callers. She walked into the lounge area and served herself coffee, taking her time. Alfredo, their lazy supervisor, wouldn't be in until noon. Dana had been trying to keep Claire's mind off of what had been bothering her, but now, sitting alone, it all came back. She sat down at the plastic lunch table holding her hot cup of coffee and looked outside the huge windows to the garden outside the building. A small squirrel ran up a tree and Claire's eyes followed it. Mexican squirrels. Marco had called them that. Mexican squirrels, because they were so small. These valley squirrels seemed to never grow, not like the big fat fluffy ones you saw on TV. New York squirrels. No, these particular squirrels were small and thin but probably somehow still managed to be diabetic, Marco had said. Claire had laughed her ass off and that image of the squirrels never left her. Every time she saw one she imagined it wearing a tiny sombrero, and it always made her think of Marco. The squirrel sightings were surprisingly rare, but that's probably what made them a little more special. Silly things. A little smile came to her face and her hand reached to her pocket to feel her cell phone.

But she wouldn't call him. Many times a day she thought of her friend Marco, but she called him nowhere near as many times as she really wanted to. She was afraid to. Afraid of moving forward, afraid becoming vulnerable to him, afraid of being honest with him and almost certainly losing him because her honesty would be too little, too late. The squirrel climbed around to the other side of the tree and it was gone. Her smile left with it.

She kept her hand on her phone. Marco used to call her a lot when they first started talking. The first few times she answered frequently and promptly, but the more they spoke and the more they saw each other, the more distant she became. She had to. The closer they got the more she felt that if she would keep her distance from him while giving a little, just enough of herself, the more she could string their friendship along. She hated putting it like that but it was the truth. Maybe she could keep it going and never mention to Marco how much she had wanted to not give a damn about him. But she was afraid, and she was never afraid. It was only with Marco that she felt trepidation about saying what she really meant to say. There was Dana of course, but that was different. Dana was a great friend and a wonderful lover when she needed one, but there was no pretension about possibly being together, from either of them. They loved each other deeply, but they had never been in love with one another.

Her thoughts returned to that night she met Marco, and to Dave. No guy had ever hit her before. Nobody had dared. She didn't think that could have ever happened to her, much less so to let the bastard get away with it. But that's what she had essentially done. She didn't press charges. She just told him to fuck off, and fuck off he did, although she suspected that he was much more afraid of Dana than he was of her. No one at all messed with Dana. Dana would thoroughly hurt someone, and she very impatiently waited for Claire to give her the go to put the hurt on Dave. She vaguely thought about what Dana would actually do to Dave and shook her head. Something very, very bad indeed.

A dim consideration crossed her mind. Maybe she deserved to get hit. Maybe that punch to the side of her face and the ringing in her ear were karma coming back to bite her. Maybe she had deserved her sore jaw. No, she had never cheated on Dave or done anything to betray his trust. She had done her best to be good to him. She knew that. The same, however, couldn't be said about her previous relationships. She hadn't been a saint, not by any stretch of the imagination. She had made many a boy cry. She hadn't been someone who slept around with her boyfriend's best friend, and she was never into expensive jewelry or name brand clothing or any of the things that other women worshipped.

What she had been, frankly, was a bitch, an angry self-diagnosed bipolar bitch who rejected the simple pleasures of what guys would try to give her. Before Dave, they all had been – while not saints themselves – generally nice to her. They were mostly good to her and she treated them like dirt. Why was she like that? She remembered the kindest of them; his name was Jeffrey. He was shorter than her, and chubby. He had come up to her during their lunch break in high school and he bravely asked her to go out. She agreed and soon they began "dating." Jeffrey followed her around like a doting puppy and, without really thinking of it, that's how she began treating him. Like a goddamn puppy. She crossed the line one day when she was talking with Dana among a small group of students. Jeffrey had just entered through the glass doors when he saw her and started heading her direction with that innocent puppy look on his face. He raised his hand to wave and – for whatever reason – Claire absently patted her legs and with cold eyes started cooing, "Here Jeffy, Jeffy! Come, boy..."

Jeffrey's face sank, and within her, almost simultaneously, Claire felt her heart sink as well. Jeffrey gave her a look of combined sadness, disgust, and disappointment. Then he turned and walked back out where he came from. Everyone close enough to hear what she had said began laughing. Claire didn't even like those people who were laughing, and for an idiotic moment she felt the need to defend Jeffrey even though the ridicule had been solely her fault. Everyone but Dana laughed at what she had said and done to Jeffrey. Dana refused to let Claire be like those other girls. She saw the good in Claire even when Claire herself didn't. She believed Claire to be better than that. Jeffrey, in his own way, was as much an outcast as Claire and Dana, and he had done nothing to deserve to be treated like dirt, especially by her own friend. She wouldn't have it. Dana, even if she wasn't friends with Jeffrey, understood him well enough. He was supposed to be one of their own, a pariah among the popular. Even if you didn't unite with others of the same ilk, a pariah did not publicly execute another pariah. It was an unspoken rule. Dana glared at Claire and walked away. Claire cursed herself under her breath and went after her. They went into the girl's bathroom and stood in front of the mirrors. They were alone. Dana was giving

Claire a look normally reserved for people whose asses she was about to kick. Claire leaned against a sink, arms crossed, eyes downward.

"What the hell is your problem?" Dana said.

Claire shrugged her shoulders and said nothing. She knew exactly what she had done, but she didn't want to deal with it just then.

"Claire."

"Look I'm sorry okay? I don't know why I did that."

"That's fucked up."

"I know, damn it. I know. I'll apologize to him later. Look, it's just he's been getting on my nerves, following me around all the fucking time. It just started annoying me."

Dana raised her hands in the air, frustrated. "Why the hell did you bother giving him the light of day then? You know you have no interest whatsoever in him. Why didn't you tell him you have a boyfriend or something? You wouldn't have to be a bitch about it, and you sure as hell didn't have to be one now."

Jeffrey's face, as his expression had gone from happiness to disgust in a matter of about two seconds, was ingrained in Claire's mind. That was all she could see as she was being reprimanded by Dana, his chubby face draining of color, and of belief in her, in his idea of Claire. *God, what a bitch.* She apologized to him the following day. Jeffrey said nothing, only nodded and kept walking to his next class. This cold shoulder from the boy who had been doting on her incessantly. She called after him but he didn't turn or acknowledge her in any way. She knew she deserved that. In a strange way she was kind of proud of him. Jeffrey deserved better. But the look on his face refused to leave her. She didn't know then how meaningful that event would become in the future. Jeffrey's sad image in the hallway – for better or worse – would become part of her.

So when she met Dave at a party she didn't really want to attend to begin with, she told herself she would change, that she wouldn't be cruel to anyone who didn't deserve it. Her guilt over her past relationships, but especially about her terrible treatment of poor Jeffrey, blinded her to the truth about what kind of person Dave really was. But it was something she failed to notice until the situation was getting out of control, until it was too late. She had stubbornly refused to listen to Dana's advice and warnings about him.

She thought the relationship had started decently enough. Dave had been...pleasant to her. But the more she looked back the more she realized how foolish she had been. He was kind enough, at first. So long as things went his way, so long as Claire did what he asked. But when Claire said she wanted to do something else, or she said she wanted to have a girl's night with Dana, he would get quiet and act hurt, act almost physically wounded. That's how it started, but when Claire began saying "no" more often, Dave's outbursts turned from fake hurt to real anger. He became louder, obnoxious, insulting. He screamed right to her face, accusing her of being selfish and of being a bitch. At first she would just stand there and take it. She started believing that this was Jeffrey somehow exacting vicarious vengeance upon her.

When Dana found out about the verbal abuse she told Claire to leave him; she didn't need garbage like him in her life. She said Claire was tougher and better than that, and she had never taken shit from men in her life and that she sure as hell didn't need to start now. But Claire wouldn't listen and she willingly kept taking Dave's verbal abuse and accusations. The relationship quickly deteriorated but she did nothing until the night outside the mall. Dana's words were finally getting through, and she was in no mood for any of Dave's idiotic outbursts. When he began screaming at her again she was at her wit's end. Dave was shocked that Claire would dare talk back to him. The condescending look of indignation in his eyes that Claire would presume to think she was his equal raised her own anger level to critical, boiling red. *That's what this asshole thinks? That's how he really feels about me, the unfaithful, self-righteous asshole? I'll show him.* So finally, her weeks of pent-up rage exploded out of her and she let loose with her own set of expletives and insults. Dave's face went wild with rage and she liked it. She felt good at having control again. Her independent take-no-shit-from-anyone attitude returned in full force. No more would she take anything from this prick. She would get out of his car for the last time, walk inside and call Dana. She would tell Dana what she finally did and her friend would be proud of her and the two of them would spend the night drinking wine and celebrating worthless Dave's departure. Of course, it didn't turn out quite that way. Dave hit her. The useless son of a bitch actually punched her. She and Dana would spend that night talking about Dave, but not how she had intended it. Dana mostly threatened to kill or seriously hurt Dave, and practically begged Claire to press charges against him and damn near lost her mind when Claire refused to do so.

By the time Dana had started nearly erupting with rage over what happened to her friend, Claire's thoughts had fallen into a quagmire. She was resentful and amazed that Dave had the gall to ever question her at all. He had no right. He gave that up when he began treating her like some kind of inferior animal. He went miles beyond the line when he slept with someone else and then somehow, someway, felt that it was perfectly okay to raise a hand to her. *Motherfucker! He thinks I've fucked someone else? Then I goddamn will fuck someone else and make sure he knows about. I'll become, at least once, what he thinks I am. It's just what he deserves.*

And then she met Marco. And the plans swimming in her head as they were at that point dissolved like fine grains of sand in someone's hand as water fell upon it. When she met Marco she tried telling herself to stick to her original, simple plan of revenge against Dave. But the way Marco was with her, so sweet and respectful – she couldn't hurt him. Marco reminded her of Jeffrey at first, and she thought that her trepidation about using and forgetting him was due to that alone; that she only liked and enjoyed him because Marco and Jeffrey were similar, and that she was only attempting to make up for her past in a small way. It felt like a sort of confusing, depressing atonement. She had somehow deserved her abuse at the hands of Dave because of what she had done to Jeffrey. And now, this complicated situation with Marco seemed to be further confirmation of circumstances coming full circle to spite her.

But beyond their general politeness, Claire knew, Marco and Jeffrey weren't that alike, not really. Marco had started to make her feel like neither Jeffrey nor Dave ever did, or could. She longed to see Marco but she began making a point of avoiding him. She would get her phone to call him but wouldn't hit send. When he called her, she would become happy and excited, but at the same time she would feel guilty and miserable. She was afraid to answer, afraid to be happy with him because it would be based on a lie, because she had desperately wanted Marco to mean nothing to her, mean less than Dave, less than anything really. Yet she knew she was only fooling herself and she knew no other solution. So she would stare at her phone until its LCD screen read "1 missed call." Before long his calls became less and less frequent, and eventually he seemed to rely on her calling him instead. He never said no to her and he always seemed so happy to see her. She felt lower than dirt. He must get frustrated about it, she thought. He had to. Maybe he felt used, but he never showed it. He steadfastly remained her Marco, sweet Marco who always tried to make her smile. She wasn't brave enough to tell him how much that was beginning to mean to her.

She looked down at her cup of coffee, now completely cold. How long was she sitting there? She checked her phone...*holy crap*! It was almost noon. Alfredo would be pulling up any minute now. She half jumped out of the chair and threw the cold coffee down the sink and jogged back to her workstation. Dana saw her come in and palmed her microphone to mute her caller. "Where the hell have you been? I was about to send search dogs after you, jerk."

Claire didn't say anything. She only glanced at Dana and did her best approximation of a small smile and started adjusting papers on her desk as she put on her headset and sat down. Dana was completely ignoring her caller as she watched Claire. "You okay, sweetie?"

"Uh-huh," Claire nodded. She checked her phone and prepared herself for the coming verbal assaults. The blinking orange lights were fully lit with callers impatiently waiting to blow their tops in the name of customer service.

Marco had no idea how to feel that morning as he got up to go to work. The same feelings of disbelief, disappointment and exhilaration melted into a giant pot of confusion, stirring themselves more and more until there weren't any single ingredients left, only a bowl of bewilderment for him to try to digest. Being with Alicia again was amazing, but she had somehow gone without a trace again, which was not so amazing. He replayed the night in his head. How was it even possible? She was only a couple of feet from him when he looked away, and even then it was only for a second or two. How was it possible that she Olympic-sprinted that far that quickly? She was hardly a tall person and though fit-looking, she didn't look the part of a world class athlete. And even if she was...

He got out of bed, took a shower, and ate his breakfast in a daze, unsure if he should feel happy or sad about the whole thing. His bacon and eggs could have been dog food or sirloin; he ate without tasting anything. When he finished eating he went to the living room and turned on the television, but left the volume so low it may as well have been off. He stared at the talking heads presumably informing him about the previous night's sporting events and political arguments. When the weatherman came on he turned up the volume. Today he and Benny would be driving around the city's residential neighborhoods exchanging recycling bins. Since Thursday's consisted of them of them being outside most of the day, it was usually a good idea to know if they would be working in sunshine, freezing weather, or torrential rainfall. It was usually sunshine but you never knew. The meteorologist, James, Lawrence, a veteran who looked like the friendly overlord of the news station, started: "...Thank you, Elizabeth. Well it looks like more of the same for the Valley. Expect sunny days ahead, with highs in the lower nineties and lows in the upper seventies, with little chance of rain. Don't turn off those air conditioners! Tonight will be just as humid and muggy and warm, just as it has been since Monday. And after that it only gets warmer, so if you thought these last several days were a little toasty then you better start getting used to our usual Valley weather again. The holiday weather, as it were, is behind us now, folks..." The weatherman went on but Marco stopped listening to him and was just staring at the screen incredulously. Did he really just say that upcoming nights were going to be as warm as the last few nights? Where had this guy been? Was he kidding, warm? Marco had been freezing his ass off the last couple of nights he had been with Alicia. It had been anything but "toasty."

Marco shut the TV off and threw the remote on the carpeted floor. He lay down on the sofa and put an arm on his forehead. He was surprised. He thought he would be as frustrated as he was before when Alicia had up and vanished the first time, and after he had discovered that the note she had given him hadn't been her number. He had thought that he wouldn't see her again. But somehow, almost miraculously, he had. Of course, she did disappear yet again after that.

He checked the time. Still enough time to relax before work. He closed his eyes and started thinking about Alicia again. He had told himself that if he saw her he would ask her exactly what she meant by the note, and how she could have known about his own thoughts that night at college. It was ridiculous; that couldn't have been it, but whatever it was, he had been determined to find out. But he didn't ask. It all somehow didn't seem so important when he was with her. The questions of how and why it had all been possible – for the two of them to meet, not once but twice, completely evaporated when they were together. But why? Next time, if – no, *when* he saw Alicia again he would finally ask her what she knew, ask her to clarify everything that currently didn't make sense to him. He wanted the questions out of his head and to simply enjoy spending time with her. He had even less of an idea about how he would see her now – not so much as a note this time – but he would see her again; somehow he just knew it.

He turned and picked the remote off the floor and set it on the coffee table with the still unrolled newspaper. He picked up the paper and lay back on the sofa, tossing it in the air a couple of times. He looked at the date on the front page without unrolling it. February 2nd. It was presently the 23rd. Why was he holding on to a three-week-old copy of The Brownsville Herald? His faces twisted in slight bewilderment. The little, frail rubber band holding the paper closed waited patiently encircling it and Marco moved his hand to pull it off, but his hands refused to obey his mind and his fingers froze in place without touching the rubber band. Then, his hands clenched tightly around the paper, pressing in and slightly crushing it between his fingers. A bizarre sense of fear and rage welled within him and he cupped two fingers under the banding and forced his hand to tear it off. He tried to unroll the paper but again his stubborn fingers refused to listen. His hands began to shake as he tried to will apart the nearly month old parchment that was disturbingly defying him.

"What the fuck..."

He bent the paper harshly in half and threw it across the living room. It thumped against the wall behind the TV and fell to the floor behind it.

Marco was standing in the middle of the living room, dumbfounded, unsure if he should be afraid or just annoyed and confused. *That fucking newspaper. What the hell.* He checked the time again. It was almost time to go to work. He walked over to the area behind the TV where the paper had landed, determined to either open it up or simply chuck the cursed, outdated little bastard into the wastebasket. Either way, he was not going to spend the whole day feeling mocked by nothing more than rolled up paper.

It's just a goddamn newspaper. Don't be stupid. You're just being weird and paranoid. He looked behind the TV, and sure enough there was the newspaper, lying on the floor, rudely bent where he had crushed it and surrounded by an army of dust bunnies but still snuggly rolled into place. "You son of a bitch." He was glaring at it as if disappointed by its contempt. He picked it up again and threw it on the sofa. It was time to leave.

He looked out the window and put his hands on the glass. It was going to be a hot day. Even this early in the morning the sun was starting to bake helpless neighborhood plants and melt the metal off of any vehicle not parked in a garage. He picked up his keys and the devil spawn of a newspaper and crushed it again between his hands. Fine. He wouldn't open it. He tried to convince himself it was a choice. He closed his apartment door and felt the sun burning down on him; work was going to be sweaty fun indeed. As he walked to his car he knew exactly what he was going to do with the newspaper. A satisfied smile crossed his face. He did work at a recycling yard after all. He got in his car and drove off.

He arrived at work at the usual time and Benny's old reliable pickup truck was there as well, early as ever. *Oh yeah*. Between thinking about Alicia and her disappearing acts and now the newspaper making him act strangely, Marco had forgotten about the unannounced cancellation of beer night with Benny. Marco hadn't talked to him at all since he saw Benny at work the day before. He thought of giving Benny a little shit for not letting him know he wouldn't make it, but changed his mind. Maybe something had happened with Lisa, something having to do with Benny and Lisa's relationship, or maybe Lisa had hit another low point concerning the death of her sister. He'd let Benny bring it up and see what had happened. If nothing seriously horrible had happened then he would pick on Benny a little. Beer night would be on Benny when they hit the bar and they would get around to the fact that they somehow didn't have each other's numbers. Or rather, why Marco hadn't given Benny his most recent number since changing service providers.

He walked inside the office and there was Benny again, making coffee. Marco waved at him and Benny did the same as best he could with a coffee pot in one hand and a mug in the other. Benny put the pot down and got an extra mug for Marco.

Marco knew something was up as soon as he was handed his mug of hot coffee. It wasn't just the look on Benny's face. Benny was being really quiet. Benny was never quiet. He went to his office and, without speaking, motioned for Marco to follow him. When they were inside the small office Benny shut the door and then sat behind his paper-strewn desk. Marco sat across from him and waited patiently.

"Hey man, I'm sorry about yesterday. I didn't mean to bail on you like that. It's just that something came up. We'll get those drinks next time okay?" For someone who was obviously in a position to not have to be so apologetic, Benny was remarkably contrite. So even if Marco had been seriously angry or disappointed with him, there was no way that he could have kept feeling that way. Benny was a difficult person to stay angry with. It almost felt morally wrong. But Marco was feeling neither anger nor resentment; he just wanted to know what had happened and hoped that Benny was okay.

"Don't worry about it. I mean, you're my boss; you don't really owe me an explanation here. Besides I'm sure you had something important to do, and whatever it was, you know, I just hope you got it taken care of. So like you said, we can always do this some other time, no rush." He wanted to ask what exactly had happened but he left the issue to Benny's discretion. He didn't want to get involved beyond what would be volunteered to him. He sipped his coffee and waited for Benny to either tell him the story or to be sent away to get the work day started. Benny nodded and was quiet for a moment before finally confiding to Marco.

"After I finished my business stuff I was about to come back here to help you close up and go for some beer, but just before I got back I got a call from Lisa. It was about her sister. I thought Lisa was doing a little better, you know? But she calls me bawling her eyes out and I could barely understand a word she's saying. She said she left her job early because she said she thought she would have some sort of nervous breakdown because she kept thinking about her sister and about how she died, and that her death was somehow her fault. I tried to tell her that there was no way she could have known. But then she was going on about how she never got to know her sister very well at all, and that she had no idea her sis' could ever have..." He shook his head.

Marco felt a pain for Benny. He had never seen him so troubled by anything. He was always so...jolly.

"Benny...how did her sister die? You never told me what happened. I wanted to ask before but I figured it was none of my business." Benny nodded again.

"She committed suicide. The night she died she told Lisa that she was going out and that she would return later that night. That was the last time they saw each other but they spoke again that night on the phone. Lisa called to ask her about something and she said she noticed a strange tone in her sister's voice. She let slip that she was staying at a Holiday Inn. Then the line got cut and Lisa began to worry. She said she had never heard her sister sound so tired. That's what she said she sounded like. Tired, but in a different way. Lisa waited for her to call or come back home, but she never did. She ended up going to the hotel and somehow convinced an employee to let her into her sister's room. Lisa found her on the bed and she said she thought her sister was sleeping but that it didn't look right. Then she saw the empty bottle of sleeping pills."

Benny's eyes went bloodshot and he was quiet a moment. "Lisa feels like it's her fault. She blames herself for her sister's death. I tell her that she couldn't have known, that she did all she could. I just hate seeing her like this. I can't imagine what she's going through after losing her baby sister. Poor Jane. I don't know what made her choose to do that. But what I do know is that it wasn't Lisa's fault. She couldn't possibly have known that Jane would kill herself."

So Jane was Lisa's sister's name. Jane. "Benny, I'm sorry, I had no idea." He shook his head and looked at Benny consolingly. "Yeah forget the whole drinking thing; you just do what you need to do. I don't really know Lisa, but tell her I'm sorry about Jane. I'm sure she was a wonderful person, and if she could somehow hear her, I'm sure Jane would know how much her sister loves and misses her."

16

Marco kept the beat up newspaper in his backpack he used for work. The little bastard would be spared the bale machine unless he and Benny made it back to the recycling yard before they normally closed up shop. Being the only recycling yard in town meant that there wasn't exactly much competition locally, but it also meant that he and Benny were in sole charge of handling the city's recycling week after week and that also meant that every single week Marco would have a veritable mountain of shredded paper and other recyclable materials to feed to the hungry bale machine. It could be hard to keep up but it was a fun challenge. He wondered how Benny had managed to do it all when he was working alone. He turned to see Benny in the driver's seat as he was driving down Central Avenue and he got his answer. Benny loved what he did. Simply loved it. He was in love with his giant beast of a work truck and he damn near pampered the thing. Since Benny's Recycling Center was the only one of its kind for miles, Marco had no way of accurately comparing it to anything, but he thought that if the city was flooded with other recycling companies, Benny's would still be the most efficient. Certainly the most loved. He looked out the passenger window. Next stop was the local middle school.

"Okay, here we are!" Benny said. "Let's roll!" Marco turned over to him and smiled and jumped out of the giant truck.

"Fuck this job," Claire said under breath after ending another annoying call from a clueless caller. She yawned and stretched and bit the tip of her pen, staring absently at her computer screen and hoping to god that she wouldn't get many more calls that day. Dana looked over at her and gave her an encouraging smile. Claire smiled back without really looking at her. Dana was worried, Claire knew, and she looked down at her desk and pretended to write something on her notepad. She didn't want to worry Dana; it only made herself feel worse.

Claire had managed to get back to her workstation just before Alfredo walked through the door. Nobody liked him, neither as a boss or really even as a person. She might have almost felt bad for him but he was so damn annoying and lazy to boot. He would typically arrive late yet still had the gall to check everyone's time cards to make sure that they punched in on time and god help you if you didn't. It wasn't that Alfredo was intimidating; he was simply longwinded every time he opened his mouth. He could make you fall asleep while standing in front of him. You'd rather watch paint dry than listen to him drawl on and on. Plus he always smelled like pasta. That he always liked to stand just a little too closely as he talked to you didn't help matters any.

But maybe she was just feeling extra angsty. She did her best to put her pasta-smelling boss out of her thoughts and looked back at Dana. She scribbled a note on a paper and tore it out. Tossed it at Dana. It bounced off the top of her head and landed on her desk. She looked at Claire.

"What the hell?"

Claire laughed quietly. "Read it!" she mouthed at Dana.

Dana opened the note and read it. *Let's go for a drive after work. Get some wine and just go somewhere. Yes or no*? She looked back up to Claire and made a weird face, shaking her head. She wrote on the note and tossed it back to Claire. Claire opened it and laughed out loud. *Bitch, what are we, in junior high? What's with the fucking notes? But yes, of course, yes. Love you*! Claire looked up and saw Dana blow a kiss at her. She returned the kiss and Dana caught it and held it to her heart dramatically. Claire laughed louder and then saw Alfredo standing outside his office looking at them, arms crossed in front of him.

"Something so funny that it's worth stopping taking calls for?" he said. Dana rolled her eyes. Claire said nothing and went back to work. Alfredo went back into his office. Claire remembered why nobody liked him.

As Benny and Marco walked down the halls of the school, Benny was quieter than usual. He was his friendly self, but much more reserved. He looked at Marco and was glad for the company, but he wanted nothing more than to take the rest of the day off and go see Lisa. She had been pretty broken up the last time he saw her. Benny had thought that Lisa was slowly but surely getting beyond the worst part of her grief, but losing someone as close as a sister can't be something one just moves on from, perhaps no matter how much time has passed. Lisa had looked so heartbroken and beaten that it broke his own heart to see her so vulnerable. Benny was falling in love with her but it was far from the right time to be laying that extra weight on her. Lisa didn't need that and he wouldn't burden her with it. He knew how much her little sister had meant to her and how much she would always love her; he could hear it in her voice and see it in her eyes when she talked about her beautiful younger sister. And she *was* beautiful. Lisa had shown him a photo of her with Jane, the two hugging and smiling, happy. The picture was taken inside of a bookstore. Apparently they had managed to get a stranger to snap the photo. Lisa said that it was the only recent photo of the both of them since their parents died. *Christ*. Two dead parents and now a dead younger sister. There were no other siblings; Lisa was completely alone now. *No, not quite alone...I'm still here, whatever it may mean.*

Benny recalled the utter solitude that he had felt when his wife had died of the aneurysm. The only solace during that horrible time was the knowledge that Amy probably didn't suffer much and that it was at least a quick death. But dead was dead, and his wife was gone forever. Benny's own parents were both gone as well at the time of his wife's fatal attack, but at least he still had his brothers, even if they were far away in different states. At least they were still around. Lisa had no one except him now. He hoped that that was enough.

"What's up, Benny?" Marco was leaning against a recycling bin, watching him. "You okay?" They were stopped in the middle of a hallway and Marco was waiting for him. Benny didn't know how long he had lingered there alone with his thoughts. He shook his head to snap out of it.

"Yeah. Yeah I'm fine, sorry." He gave Marco a hand with the bins and they kept working.

Lisa sat at the edge of the bed in her little sister's room, hands cusped between her knees and staring at the head of the otherwise empty bed, the bed that would never again be slept upon by her beautiful baby sister. She would never again get to tell her she loved her; never again hug her; never again get to argue; never again get to see the lovely face of her sweet, quiet little sis'. Her eyes watered and she felt a hot tear roll down her cheek. Her lips trembled and she could no longer hold the anguish that now exploded out of her in gushing tears. She began to shake as she sobbed uncontrollably and she put her hands to her mouth trying to stifle her cries, but she cried louder than she had cried in her life. She lay back on her sister's bed and grabbed one of the pillows and hugged it hard against her chest, holding on to it as though it was her baby sister in her arms. "I'm so sorry...I would have done anything for you. Why didn't you say anything? Why?"

She shook and sobbed into the pillow until she was exhausted and couldn't physically cry any more. After a long time she finally managed to fall asleep on her late sister's bed.

17

Claire cracked the passenger window of the Neon and rested her head against the side of the door. She liked the soothing feeling of the cooling air as it hit her face and made her hair whip back and forth against her cheeks and neck. She looked out at the passing landscape as it flashed by, occasionally looking back to get a last quick glimpse of a walking dog or a random landmark that caught her attention. She breathed in deep, almost exasperated breaths and didn't realize she was doing so, her chest moving in and out in almost cartoon-like quality.

Dana had been catching glimpses of Claire as she drove, and she thought that her friend looked absolutely adorable. It was rare to see Claire in such a state; Claire wasn't a girly girl. The only time Dana ever saw Claire be sweet was to her, but that was unique; their bond was special and forged over years of spending time together and learning to trust each other. Calling Claire a sister would have been gross since they were occasional lovers as well as friends, but labeling their bond as a simple friendship seemed inadequate, and inserting the word "best" in front of the word "friends" seemed lazy and equally lacking verisimilitude. Dana would have called Claire a sort of soul mate but neither of them liked the term to begin with. No matter. Whatever they chose to call themselves was beside the point really. They loved each other unreservedly and without having the need to say it out loud, though they frequently would. Dana moved her right hand from the stick shift and reached for Claire's left hand. Claire turned to her and smiled sweetly, and they entwined their small fingers tightly around each other's hands as they drove.

They had punched out of work several minutes early, not bothering to let Alfredo know. He would probably just have talked them to death and keep them there until it was actually time to punch out and maybe even a little later, which would have totally defeated the purpose of trying to escape from work early. A few of their coworkers gave them dirty looks but they didn't care. They knew better than to mess with Claire and Dana. The only reservation came from Claire. They had already been given the stink eye from Alfredo earlier and she didn't want to push their luck by also punching out early. Dana had grabbed both of their cards and smiled at Claire and pretended to listen to her as Claire went on about it not being such a good idea. Dana looked right at her, nodding and grinning and punched both of them out anyway. Claire stopped speaking but her mouth remained awkwardly half open midsentence, her face with a look of both disbelief and also *why am I even surprised*?

Dana laughed and put an arm around Claire's shoulder and then gently patted her lower back to move her along. "Come on, let's go," Dana said, smiling. "Let's get an early start on that wine."

They had stopped at the nearest liquor store and bought a bottle of Merlot and a fresh pack of Camel cancer sticks. They decided to go to Boca Chica beach, further down the road from where Marco worked. It had been Dana's idea to go there and Claire didn't object; Dana knew she wouldn't. As they approached the right turn to head to the beach and were about a mile away from driving by Marco's job, Dana looked over at Claire and gently tugged her hand in the direction of the recycling yard. "You know you want to look," Dana said.

"Shut up." Claire glared at Dana and she smiled because Claire did look over. She hoped to catch a glimpse of Marco doing whatever it was he did at his job. They both scanned the area as the slowly drove by without luck. Marco and his boss were probably both out somewhere.

"You want me to go back? We can always park outside the gate and wait for him to show his pretty face," Dana said.

"No! You better not. Keep driving."

"You're so cute. I don't know what it is about him, Claire. You're never like this. It's adorable really."

"Shut up."

They arrived at the beach a few minutes later. Dana parked on the side of the sandy road a few hundred yards in. There were hardly any cars or people walking around.

"Want to go for a walk or just hang out here?" Dana asked.

"Let's just hang here and drink in the car. I don't feel like walking."

"Yes, ma'am. Lazy ass." Dana pulled out the wine opener and popped the cork off easily. "Ah shit," she said. "You realize we didn't bring any glasses? Or even cups."

Claire reached over and took the bottle from Dana and took a giant swig right from the bottle. She wiped her lips and returned the bottle to Dana.

"Or we can do that," Dana said. "You savage."

Claire raised her eyebrows. "Oh now you're the wine expert? I was the one who introduced you to wine in the first place, bitch." She held out her hand for the wine bottle. "If you don't want any I'll be happy to drink it by myself and you can watch."

"Don't call me a bitch, bitch," Dana said. "Marco wouldn't appreciate that dirty mouth of yours." She stared at Claire's lips. "Then again maybe he would," she said, winking and taking a huge gulp of the wine herself.

"Oh shut up. Jerk."

Dana gave her a flirty look. "Okay, okay...so you ready to tell me what's up or do we need to finish this to loosen you up a bit?"

Claire sighed. "I'm honestly not sure how much there is to tell. He's moving on I think and I don't know that I have much of a right to say anything other than I am happy for him."

"Are you?"

Claire shrugged and said nothing.

"You're obviously not. And we both know why. But the problem is you won't admit it to him. Shit you won't even admit it to yourself really."

"Admit what."

"Oh come off it, Claire. Honestly. Why can't you just say it? He's the only person you get all mushy about but you don't want to admit the obvious. He's the only person you get defensive about and just about the only person you bring up in conversation who you don't bash on. Just say it. Out loud."

"No."

"Why the hell not?"

"I can't."

"What are you-?"

"I don't deserve him! All right?" She took the bottle from Dana but didn't drink any, just held it between her legs as she turned in her seat to face Dana. Her face was devoid of any humor for the first time.

"Since when are you so melodramatic about anything? What is this about, Claire? Your ex-boyfriends? Don't tell me this is about Jeffrey?"

Claire was quiet at that.

Dana sat back in her seat with a thump and threw her head back. "Oh my god, Claire. That is what this is about isn't it? You're still hung up on that crap aren't you? You have to let that go. Jeffrey is in the past, so are all the other guys you were ever with. It's done. Forget all that. What the hell, Claire."

"You told me yourself that I had been a bitch about that, Dana."

"You *were* a fucking bitch. *Were*, okay? People change. And it doesn't have to be in extremes. You don't have to be an asshole, but you don't have to make a 180 degree turn and end up in the position that you did with Dave either. Your past mistakes don't have to become your future punishments, and it doesn't justify other people treating you like shit. It also doesn't mean that you have to treat yourself like crap either."

"No? And what about karma?"

"Fuck karma. That's all bullshit and you know it. Besides, if karma did actually work, I don't think it would be fair to punish people who really did have regrets about the fucked up shit they may have done in the past. Bad karma would be for people who truly aren't remorseful about anything and just kept on hurting others just because they could, or because they liked it. Like that fucker Dave. He can go to hell."

Claire laughed a little at that last part. "You think so?"

"Yeah, Claire, I do. You know, we can always regret things, but for how long? I think the more important thing to focus on is not regret about anything, but in trying to change things about yourself that you think aren't good or that you don't like. But for yourself." She took the wine from Claire and handed it back after an enormous drink from the bottle. "Just keep moving ford."

"Ford?"

"What?" Dana said.

"You just said to keep moving ford..." Claire felt the bottle in her hands and shook it a little. "Holy shit, Dana! You finished it! I think I'll be the one driving home if you don't mind."

"Sure. Sorry I finished the wine."

"It's okay," Claire said, smiling once again. She switched seats with Dana.

"You just make me drink so much because you're high maintenance and needy," Dana said.

Claire leaned over and hugged her and kissed her on the cheek. "Come on, dork, let's go home."

"Okay."

"And thank you."

"Anytime, love."

Claire got the empty bottle and scanned the beach for the nearest trash can. She spotted one a short distance from the car and walked over to it to discard the bottle. Don't mess with Texas, and all that. When she dunked the bottle in the trash can she looked up and in the distance she saw the silhouette of a pickup truck. It wasn't parked off of the side of the road like it was supposed to be; it looked to be simply idling in the middle of the path, facing the Neon's direction. Claire brushed the hair out of her eyes and squinted through her glasses to try to get a better view of the truck, but it was too far away to see it very well, much less check to see if someone was just sitting in the cab and looking at her and Dana. *How long had that truck been there? Had it been there before they arrived and they somehow just failed to spot it*? Well, they had been drinking and had better things to worry about anyway. She put the truck from her mind and returned to the Neon to head back home. Dana was already asleep in the passenger seat. Claire grinned. *And she thinks I'm cute.* She turned the key in the ignition and the car came to life. She drove onto the main beach access road and looked in the rearview mirror for a last curious glance at the pickup truck getting smaller in the distance. She was pretty sure that the truck hadn't been there when they had arrived.

As Claire and Dana left the sandy road of the beach and turned onto the concrete street that led home, the lights of the pickup truck flashed brightly in the quickly darkening sky and the V8 engine screamed to life in the mostly empty beach, sand rising violently in the air from the powerful exhaust. A scarred over and arthritic-looking right hand reached for the gear shift and moved it from Park to Drive and the blue Chevy Silverado drove in the direction that the Neon had gone.

18

Claire couldn't help taking another look at the recycling yard as she drove back home. She didn't really expect – and didn't get – a lucky glimpse of Marco, but it didn't hurt to try. All she saw was Dana in the foreground, fast asleep in her seat. She was happy they had gotten to talk a little; it was only right. Dana deserved to know what was going on with her, and Claire thought that she had done a decent job of trying to convey to her friend feelings that she herself hadn't quite understood too well. It was difficult trying to process those feelings in her mind, much less elucidate them. But Dana was good at getting to the bottom of things and even if it annoyed Claire sometimes, she knew that Dana meant well and that she was right most of the time, besides. She owed Dana her gratitude. If she didn't have her to share her bottled up emotions with, she was quite sure she would never talk to anyone else about how she was feeling about *anything*. She would probably keep everything inside until she would one day just blow up and likely do something very, very stupid like get herself arrested or choosing to stay with Dave until she ended up killing the bastard and thus getting herself arrested.

Claire let out a heavy breath and rested back against her seat. She smoked a cigarette as she thought of what to do next. She knew that she had to talk to Marco. She had to tell him how she felt even though she was afraid to do so. She thought and hoped that she was only exaggerating the ramifications of having lied to him at the beginning of their friendship. It was a strange feeling when they met. She had never wanted so badly for someone to be just a little bit of a jerk, or at least an annoying cocky fool. But Marco had been kind and felt like a genuine person; what he said was what he meant. And it had felt like an effortless connection of the minds somehow. She hadn't planned to smile that night. She hadn't expected to feel any kind of happiness and it came as a shock that Marco brought that out of her, even a little bit. She had felt as happy as a just physically abused person could possibly feel, and that was quite the fucked up emotional state to have been in. Marco had been the right guy but at the wrong time. Many a time, when the two were alone drinking together she had wanted to straddle and kiss him and make drunken love with him, but the thought always in her mind that took precedence was, *Sweetie, why couldn't I have met you sooner? You have no idea what I'm feeling for you; you don't know what it's like wanting to tell you that I want you and that I'm falling for you; you don't know how much more I'd like to see you than I actually do,* and then...*You don't know that I originally wanted nothing to do with you; that you were supposed to be a one and done sort of deal; you don't know that I had led you on before I really knew anything about you; you don't know that I used to be a bitch and treat guys like you like disposable things. You don't know how much of a bitch I used to be and maybe I still am, and maybe I'm just afraid that I'll revert to my old ways and just emotionally fuck you up when I know you don't deserve it. Because I'm poison...*

When that train of thought rolled through her mind she knew she had finally truly understood her reticence about coming clean to Marco. It wasn't only fear that Marco wouldn't understand what she was going through. It wasn't merely worry that he would feel used or betrayed by her. She was just as fearful of becoming who she had been before she went out with Dave. She was afraid, as Dana had told her, to do the easy thing and do a complete U turn and revert to her old ways. She was wary of treating Marco like nothing, like poor Jeffrey. She didn't know whether Jeffrey had ever forgiven her, and she never saw him again to ask him. Her hands gripped the steering wheel tightly and her knuckles were white against the leather cover. She didn't want to think of the possibility of completely severing ties with Marco, never to see him again. Selfish or not, she didn't want that to happen.

Dana was right. Of course she was right. A feeling of hope came across her face as she thought of telling Marco how she felt, but it evaporated just as quickly. That's right. He's met someone. She fought the urge to use that as an excuse to not talk to him. She was tired of pretending to only care about him as a friend. He had a right to the truth and she couldn't keep it inside her any longer. She would call him tomorrow. Whatever happened or didn't happen with Marco's new girl friend wasn't any of her business, but she would finally tell him how she felt about him. If it turned out that Marco and this new girl were getting serious and that meant that she had to back off and remain only friends with him, then so be it. However badly it may hurt her, if it came to that, she would remain his friend and try to be happy for him. Strangely, the thought occurred to her that this other girl better be pretty, but not too pretty. She laughed quietly at the silly thought.

Tomorrow. She would call Marco tomorrow and ask him to hang out after work. She would bite the bullet and tell him everything as best as she could. She put out her cigarette and lit another one as she reached above her to adjust the rearview mirror. Far off in the distance, very faintly, she could see the headlights of another vehicle driving down the same road.

19

"Another round?" Benny asked Marco.

"Sure," Marco said, smiling and lighting a cigarette. He was starting to get buzzed, but he was having too much fun with Benny to decline a bucket of Dos Equis. "Bring 'em on."

"Man, Marco, we should have done this sooner. It sure is nice to be able to talk about something not having to do with recycling shit huh?"

"Sure, Benny, but don't try to lie to me. You're probably thinking about throwing these beer bottles in a bag and taking them back to the shop."

"The thought did cross my mind."

The bucket arrived and they dug into it for a couple of more beers. Marco opened his beer and looked at Benny. He didn't want to turn beer night into a somber occasion, but he judged it against not asking the question he was about to ask and decided that bringing up the situation with Lisa was probably the best thing to do. He didn't want Benny to think that he didn't care.

"So, how is Lisa, Benny? Don't take this the wrong way, but I thought that maybe you'd want to be over there with her right now."

"Well, don't take *this* the wrong way, Marco, but I *would* rather be with her right now," he said as he took a sip of beer. He set it down on the table and his face took on a more serious expression. "I did talk to her earlier. She said that she felt more or less okay, but that she wanted to be alone for awhile. She also asked me to not take *that* the wrong way. I guess it's a day of not taking things the wrong way huh? Anyway, I said I understood but I told her to call me if she needed anything, know what I mean? I want to see her but I don't want to see her depressed, though I can hardly blame her for it."

"I understand what you mean. You want to see loved ones but you don't want to see them in pain."

"Exactly."

They sat in silence for a moment and listened to the sounds of the jukebox and the other customers in the bar. The bar was mostly empty; it was a weekday after all, and the mood in the bar was very lax except for the sounds of Pantera blasting from the jukebox. Whoever had sacrificed his hard earned dollar to the jukebox god had chosen a long series of heavy metal songs. Marco approved. He allowed himself a moment to enjoy a blistering solo from the late

Dimebag Darrell before resuming his conversation with Benny, who broke the silence near the end of one of the songs.

"And what about the girl you met? How's that going?"

Very strangely and kind of wonderfully, he thought. He almost said it but instead he said, "Pretty well. She's something all right..." He would not tell Benny about her mysterious disappearing acts or even the full truth about the ways he kept meeting her. He couldn't tell him that lest Benny think him a bit crazy. Maybe he was a little.

"She's gorgeous," Marco said. She's different but in a great way. There's something about her that's...intriguing. It's weird. I still don't know much about her but I want to know, probably more than I can explain. Do you know what I mean?"

Benny nodded. "I hear ya." That's great, man. What's her name anyway? You haven't even told me."

"Oh yeah. Her name's Alicia." Just the mention of her name made him smile, but soon enough the smile went away when he saw Benny's expression.

Benny had a beer halfway to his lips but his hand froze in that position. He looked down at the table and set the beer down, shuffling it around lazily. Marco was no longer smiling and he set his own beer down as well. "What's wrong?" he said.

Benny shook his head slowly. "Nothing. Sorry about that. Just...coincidences." He took a drink of beer.

"What do you mean? What coincidences?"

"It's not the kind of coincidences to share or celebrate. It's just surprising I guess. But I don't want to go there. Forget it?" The look on Benny's face said that it really wasn't a question, so Marco dropped the issue.

"All right. It's cool."

Benny nodded his gratitude, but as much as he had wanted to keep the mood light and forget the subject that came up it was impossible to miss that the tone of the conversation had taken a downturn. They made small talk but it wasn't the same as it was minutes before. When the music playing switched over from hard rock to modern country they decided to call it a night. Benny paid the tab. Marco argued about it briefly but Benny wouldn't have it, so he settled on leaving the tip instead and they walked over to their vehicles.

"Tomorrow then, Marco! This was fun, we should do this again."

"You got it, boss," Marco said, and waved goodbye to Benny. He got in his own car and sat there with the ignition off for a few minutes, thinking things over. He thought that he would definitely have more drinks with Benny in the future; he thought about Claire; he thought about Alicia...and wondered. For some time he had harbored romantic thoughts about Claire. She was beautiful and could be sweet in her own faux-evil way. She was a rebel of sorts, someone who was different and didn't take crap from anyone. She was equally tough and pretty and uniquely wonderful, even though she wasn't always there for him. He was attracted to her, but somehow he never made a move and she never seemed really open to the possibility of being romantic with him. Though she never said something like it, she always seemed to have a defensive and invisible wall around her. He didn't want to lose Claire or get shoved aside if he was rejected, so he never took the risk. He wondered though.

He then thought of Alicia. She was an enigma to say the least. He found himself spellbound by her, by her effortless beauty and the way they would happen to find each other. It was something that felt perfect, however unbelievable it was. Probably more so because of how impossible the whole thing should have been. And Alicia had a kind of ...aura. He didn't know how else to describe it.

Then Benny came to his thoughts, how he had gone suddenly quiet and serious and wanting to change the subject. What did he mean by coincidences? He had said that after Marco had said Alicia's name, but why? There was no point just sitting in the car wondering all night. He would let Benny tell him what he meant when he felt like it. There was no point badgering him about it. He closed his eyes and yawned. He must have been more tired than he thought. He took a deep breath and opened his eyes again. He turned the key in the ignition and drove home.

-Twenty-

Look at me, Marco. LOOK at me.

No.

You know you can't win, Marco. You know where this is headed, sweetheart. Don't pretend that you don't know. You see it, Marco? Are you beginning to see the truth? Afraid to?

Please stop...

Now why would I do that? Why should I do that for you when you were given fair warning? Why should you be spared anything after you were so stubborn in continuing to ask for what you knew you would never get, what you knew that you didn't deserve? No, it's much too late for that, sweetie. It's much too late and now you're going to hear me out and this frail wall of hope and happiness that you were so set on building up will crumble to the dirt as it's always meant to. I'm doing nothing more than what you deserve and nothing less.

But why goddammit...get the hell out of my head!

Oh dear, sweet Marco. You really are a foolish little thing. You can no more get rid of me than you can your own miserable head on your shoulders. I am part of you. I AM you. We are entwined, Marco...Oh, baby...why are you shaking your head at me? Are you really so unwilling to accept the truth and realize that I'm here to stay, love?

I don't want you. I don't need you. Goddamn you, get the hell out of my mind. What the hell do you want from me? I've never asked for much...I don't need this. I don't need you in my head.

As I said my love, you can no more get rid of me than you can rid yourself of your own head, your own mind, your own subconscious. You destroy me...and you destroy yourself entirely. And oh I dare you to do that, Marco, Oh how I dare you. Pull it, so soft against your finger; Jump off, close your eyes and feel as if you have wings, falling, falling...swallow the dose, feel the oncoming sleep, inevitable; disappear the dais underneath you feet, feel the brief freefall before the sudden break, and then sway, sway...oh no tears, Marco! Can you do it? Show me; show me...It doesn't much matter to me sweet, foolish, lonely Marco. What I can tell you is this, that what you are after, the bliss, the normality and happiness you long for shall never come to pass. Why should it? Why should anyone care? Tell me, baby, I'd like to know.

Stop. You are not me. I don't need you and I can do this. I can be happy. I've found it already. I have it! You're wrong this time.

Oh, Marco. You poor baby. What is it that you think you have found? What is it that you think is within your grasp? Think hard now, but trust me that the truth isn't pleasant. It's best if you let this go now. Accept your lot, right now, this moment and all others. Because if you don't, Marco, if you don't, then I promise that you will have it so much worse than you have ever had it, so much worse than you can possibly imagine. It is better for you to trust me. Acquiesce to me and to the place you know you belong. Make it easier on yourself, love.

I owe you nothing. I'll leave you behind me.

You can NEVER leave me behind. The sooner you learn that the sooner you can stop this foolish hope of yours. It will NEVER get better, Marco. You will not find what you need. Understand that, Marco. Look at you. Look at what you are. Do you think that your parents would be proud of the thing that you are? You are a bitter disappointment. You know this.

No...

You can't argue with the truth of things, Marco. It is over. You know it. You're starting to accept it, yes.

No! I don't accept what you're saying. I don't believe you.

Foolish child. Wrong answer, Marco, very wrong. So be it. Soon the dice shall roll and you'll know that you cannot win. You shall know the truth about everything and all your luckless cards will be flat on the table. The dominoes begin their fall. Get ready for the end of the world. I warned you, sweetie...I warned you.

21

Claire had to almost carry Dana to her bedroom. She knew that Dana couldn't be *that* drunk and that she was just being difficult on purpose. When Dana literally ran through the doorway and jumped dramatically onto her bed Claire knew that that was the case. She didn't mind. It was cuter than it was annoying. Dana rolled her bed sheets over herself and became a human burrito and turned to face Claire standing in the doorway. She smiled up at her sleepily.

"Goodnight, Dana," Claire said, turning off the light and closing the door behind her.

"'Night, hon'," Dana said.

Claire walked to the kitchen to get a snack; it was way too early to go to bed. At least Dana would be plenty rested for work the next day, assuming she didn't wake up at two in the morning and unable to go back to sleep, she thought. She got a soda and made herself a quick, plain sandwich. She ate quickly, leaving her soda nearly half full and went to the living room sofa and lit a cigarette. There had been something bothering her and she was wondering if it was only her imagination.

She thought back to their trip to the beach. That truck. There was something about it. She could have sworn that it hadn't been there when she and Dana had arrived. She took a long drag of her smoke and rested her hand under her chin. The smoke quickly fogged up her glasses and she took them off and set them on her lap. The image of the idling truck on the beach remained. Well...so what if the truck arrived after them? It is a public beach after all. But people didn't generally leave their vehicles idling in the middle of the beach road. And facing their direction. Was that just a coincidence? She was probably just being paranoid. She jammed her cigarette in the ash tray and went to the living room and peered out the windows. She froze to the spot. A block down the street, adjacent to the house, was parked a Chevy Silverado. The front of their truck was pointed toward their house. If she'd had her cigarette in her mouth she would have dropped it. A heavy feeling of rage and fear filled her and she gripped the curtains tightly in her fists. Suddenly the Silverado's engine roared to life and the high beams flashed across the dark neighborhood. The Silverado did a very slow U-turn, slowing down even more as the bright lights flashed across Claire and the house, almost lingering there. Then the truck sped away, leaving smoke in the air and black marks on the concrete.

Claire remained by the window, almost shaking with an ominous feeling that she could not identify. Her fists remained fiercely gripping the curtains and she tore them down as she walked away, as if the curtains were super glued to her hands. They fell softly to the ground. She went to the front door and checked that it was locked and did the same to the remaining doors and windows. Satisfied, she got a beer from the refrigerator and started heading for her bedroom. She glanced inside Dana's room to check in on her. She was sound asleep. She locked Dana's door from the inside and shut it tight behind her and went to her room. She drank her beer on her bed and didn't manage to get any sleep for several hours.

"Where have you been?" Brenda Lopez asked, sitting up in the bed. "I've been waiting for hours. We were supposed to go out remember?"

"Don't worry about it."

"What do you mean 'don't worry about it?' Where were you?"

He threw his keys on the dresser next to Brenda. They smashed loudly against the wood and the ceramic figures atop the dresser. Brenda jumped in the bed and let out a little squeal. She dropped the subject.

"I'm sorry," she said and got out of bed. She went to the bathroom and very quietly closed the door behind her. She stood in front of the mirror, at first just staring at the floor, but then she looked up to see her reflection staring back at her. She looked pretty. At least she had looked pretty. Her face now looked haggard, the mascara running down her face in thick, inky lines. She had begun to cry. Her mouth twisted in the way it does when a person tries not to cry but ends up crying even harder. She tried to force her face to remain stoic but she failed miserably. She cupped her mouth with her hands to stifle the moaning cry she let out. She held her hands to her face and then behind her head as she cried and her body shook pitifully. She sat at the edge of the bathtub and wept as quietly as she could.

She didn't know why she put up with it. She had thought that he was a decent enough guy at first, and he wasn't bad-looking. He had been a little rough around the edges, but she thought that she could smooth them out a little, just enough so that he wouldn't become what he had become. She thought that he had an upside to him inside and she would help bring it to the light. But every time that she would bring it up and ask him why he became so angry all of the time it did little more than make him angrier still. He would yell at her and now he had taken the liberty to viciously insult her as well. He had yet to lay a hand on her and get physically abusive, but she was starting to think that it was only a matter of time. In fact, she was becoming quite sure of that. She had to get out. She had to leave him before he hurt her any further. She did not want to become a statistic; she did not want to be one of the abused who just took it and never said or did anything about it. Because she knew, somehow, that if he did ever lay a hand on her, she would become too petrified at that point to do anything. It would be too late.

She would not let it get to that point. By sheer force of will, she made the tears stop flowing and she steeled herself against the shaking. She wiped the tears away from her face with the palms of her hands and she felt the look of fear that she had had on her face change into one of determination. She would end it. Tonight. She stood and went to the mirror to see her face. She felt ready now.

There was a sudden heaving pounding at the door. Brenda jumped and she hated herself for it.

"Hurry up in there!" He said. Brenda became furious but she forced herself to remain calm. She would open the door and then have a short talk with him, tell him it was over. And that would be that. Then she would tell her friends what an asshole he was and have a good laugh at his expense for once. She looked at herself in the mirror again and was happy with her strong expression. She opened the bathroom door and walked out. He was standing close to the door with his hands in his pockets, leaning against the wall. Brenda stopped a few feet away from him, holding her ground.

"About time," he said.

"We need to talk," Brenda said as evenly as she could.

He barely acknowledged her. He smirked and got off the wall and stood frighteningly close to her for a second before walking by her and going into the bathroom, slamming the door behind him.

"Get your shit and get the fuck out," he said through the closed door.

Brenda was shocked, her eyes wide and her mouth frozen idiotically open. The sonofabitch. The motherfucking son of a bitch.

He had just told her to get lost; he had just ended it with *her*. After all that she had put up with from this asshole she wouldn't even get the chance to be the one to end it; she wouldn't get the chance to save some face or leave the bastard with any dignity. Her face contorted into one of pure rage and contempt and she went to the closed bathroom door and was about to pound on it and demand that he come out so she could chew his ass out for once and then leave. But she thought better of it. She didn't want to tempt anything by possibly making him get violent. She didn't want to get beat to hell if it wasn't even going to mean anything. It was over and that was that. She would no longer have to put up with him and that was the bigger picture.

Brenda stepped away from the door and collected her clothes and whatever belongings she had that weren't in the bathroom. She could always buy another toothbrush and more makeup. She didn't want to see his face anymore and those personal items were not nearly important enough to fuss about. She put all of her items inside a small sports bag and went to the bedroom door. She turned to the bathroom door for one final glance at the life she was about to leave forever. Her face betrayed anger and contempt, but also relief. She gripped the doorknob. She wanted to cuss him to hell on her way out but she had no energy left to do so.

Goodbye, you fucking prick.

"Goodbye, Dave," Brenda said and walked out for the last time.

"Do you want some bacon with your eggs, honey?"

Dave looked up from his plate and smiled. "Yeah, Mom." His mother returned the smile and grabbed a piece of bacon from the pan and set it on Dave's plate. Magda Robinson sat across the table from her son. She gave him a warm smile again. "Eat up. Don't let your food get cold."

Magda was surprised to see Dave drop by. He didn't visit very often, but he had showed up early in the morning. She had been out in her garden tending to her flowers and Dave pulled up out of the blue in a new Silverado. He must have sold the Mustang at some point. Dave walked up to her and gave her a hug before even saying anything. He'd even brought her flowers. She was beyond surprised. It was borderline shocking. She was thrilled to see him. Any time she got to see her only son was a reason to celebrate, especially since his visits were so rare. She almost started crying when Dave gave her the flowers. He had never done anything like that. He never showed that kind of emotion. She immediately placed her flowers in a vase with water and proudly set it on top of her kitchen table. She told Dave to make himself at home while she prepared a big breakfast for the two of them. She felt full of energy to have her boy back home again.

In the back of her mind, however, she felt an uneasy feeling, almost like a premonition or dread about something. It wasn't the fact that Dave had shown up out of nowhere and brought her flowers; at least it wasn't only that. Dave had looked tired, as if he hadn't slept a wink all night. She hoped that everything was all right. She wanted to ask him what was on his mind and find out if he needed some kind of help. He was her boy after all, but she didn't want to push him away. He was never one to open up to her, and she thought that if she looked like she was prying or interrogating him then Dave would clam up and leave again. Magda didn't want him to leave. She was so proud and happy that he was home, even if only for a little while. She wanted to prolong his visit as long as possible. She had no idea when he would visit her again. She looked at her son as he ate his breakfast and couldn't keep a smile from her face.

Dave looked up at her. "What?"

"Nothing, honey," Magda said and began eating her breakfast as well. They ate in comfortable silence. When they finished eating,

Magda got up from the table and went to pick up Dave's plate to take it to the sink and wash the dishes.

Dave put his hand over his mother's and patted it. "I got it, Mom. I'll wash them." Magda couldn't hide her look of complete shock and she put a hand on her chest, frozen in place. Dave pretended not to notice and began washing the dishes. Magda stared at him, eyes wide and on the verge of tears. She felt a tornado of emotions begin to well up inside her. She couldn't have been happier than to have her morning begin with an unexpected visit from her son, but now she was also feeling a little afraid. Dave had never acted so doting and loving to her; he had never been so kind. She didn't know how to feel. She couldn't help feeling that something had happened to her son and she wouldn't know what to do if something had actually occurred. She stood behind him in the kitchen and began to silently cry. Her son had come by to visit her and she didn't even have to ask him to. He had brought her flowers and was even cleaning up for her. Tears rolled down her face and she cupped her hands in front of her, unsure what to do. She left the kitchen before Dave could turn around and see his mother crying. She went to her bedroom and dried her tears and smiled. Davie was a good man. He had become a better man than his father ever was. Dave Sr. had left them both when little Davie was barely old enough to walk. *Look at your son now, David. Your son is a kinder, more loving person than you ever were*. Magda beamed, full of renewed hope and an endless ocean of maternal love for her only son. She went back to the kitchen. Dave had just finished washing the dishes and was drying his hands with a cloth towel. He looked at her and smiled. Magda smiled a mother's smile but began feeling a little sad as well. She knew that he had to be at work soon. He probably had to have been there by now. She looked down a little sadly and got her garden gloves and hat so she could begin the daily tending of her garden.

"Do you want some help, Mom?"

Magda again cupped her hands in the way that she did when she didn't know what else to do. "That would be wonderful, Davie, but shouldn't you be heading to work now?"

"No, Mom, I took the day off. Thought I'd spend some time here with you today. If that's okay."

Magda had to use all of her willpower to keep from crying. She nodded. "Of course, honey, I would love that."

Dave nodded toward her gloves and hat. "Are the other gloves and gardening tools still in the same place?"

Magda nodded.

"Okay. Let me grab some stuff and I'll meet you out front so I can help you with the garden."

She nodded again. "Okay, son." She went outside, smiling, prouder than she had been all of her life. *You're not half the man that your son is.*

Dave stood inside for a moment without moving, only looking to the spot where his mother had been standing. He knew that he was making his mother happy by being there, and it was breaking his heart. Sometimes he wished that his mother had abandoned him as well. That would make what he was going to do so much easier. He knew that he was going to hurt his mother more than she had ever been hurt before, worse than when she was left alone to raise her child. She didn't deserve it. She probably thought that he was a better man than his father had been. But before long he would prove her wrong. Maybe he was even worse than his father. He loved his mother and he would kill anyone who would hurt her. The irony was not lost on him. He knew that if he ever ran into his father it would not be a happy reunion. His father couldn't change who he was inside, and he chose to abandon his family. He couldn't change. And Dave figured that neither could he. Maybe he was his father's son more than he cared to believe.

He would get his revenge. He wouldn't allow anyone to make a fool of him. The thought of hurting his mother had almost caused him to go back on what he was about to do, almost made him falter. But he resolved to do it. His will had returned and he felt the anger come back in full form. He would go through with it. He was not weak and he would not be disrespected. He would make her listen, one way or another. The issue was not over until he said it was. He needed to confirm his suspicions. He looked at his right hand that had been crushed by the car door and he got even more pissed off and sure that he would do what needed to be done. She would listen to him all right. And if she didn't listen then things were not going to be pretty.

But that would wait for now. He went to the storage closet and grabbed some gloves and gardening supplies and then went outside to join his mother.

They worked in mostly silence just as they had when they ate breakfast together. Magda didn't complain a bit. She was just so happy to be with her son. He had asked for the day off to spend time with her. *I love you, son.* She wondered if Dave was still with that girl. He had only brought her once. She had seemed a feisty, spirited girl and though Magda only met her briefly, she liked her. What was her name? Claire. Yes, Claire. The only thing that worried Magda was that Claire drove a motorcycle. She hoped the poor thing drove carefully. She wanted to ask Dave about her but since he didn't mention her at all she figured maybe they had broken up. That was too bad.

She looked over at Dave. He was working deathly quiet, pulling up weeds and digging holes for fresh plants and flowers. The feeling of unease returned but she pushed it away. He was here and that's all that mattered. Around noon they finished their chores. Dave picked up all the tools and cleaned up. He forbade his mother from doing any of that work. They drank lemonade and rested for a few minutes in the kitchen.

"I guess I should be going, Mom," Dave said.

"Okay, honey. Thank you for coming by and spending time with me. It's good to know you still think about your old mom."

"Mom..."

"I know, Davie, I know. I'm not trying to make speeches. I'm only happy that's all."

Dave looked at his mother for a long time. She was a beautiful woman. Her graying hair and her hard-worked hands didn't diminish it. She was a sweet person and stronger than she knew. She deserved a better deal than she had gotten in life. His cowardly father didn't deserve to be her husband. He recognized the look of happiness and pride that she had on her face now, happiness that her child was home and pride about who and what she thought her son was. He saw her smiling at him and he knew that he didn't deserve to be her son any more than his father had deserved to be her husband. Magda Robinson deserved to have a life of joy and a wealth of good memories. Neither her husband nor her son deserved her beautiful love, not nearly. *I'm so sorry, Mom...*

Dave stood and grabbed the keys to his truck and they made their way outside. His mom walked with him with an arm lovingly around his shoulder. They stood next to the door of the Silverado for a moment, quiet.

"Thank you for coming by." She raised a hand in the air to wave goodbye to him. Dave got closer to his mother and hugged her tightly. Magda, about to cry again, hugged her son intensely. They stood embracing wordlessly for what seemed like several minutes.

They separated and they both noticed that each other's eyes were misty, but neither made mention of it. Dave jumped in the Silverado and started the truck. He rolled down the window and turned to his mother. "Love you, Mom."

Magda cried. Happiness and fear coursed through her heart and she managed a smile. "I love you too, son."

Dave drove away and his mother stood on the sidewalk for a long time. She stared off in the direction that her son had gone. It was the last time Magda saw her son alive.

23

Marco lay in bed smoking. He was on his sixth cigarette. Benny had called him earlier and told him that he didn't have to come in to work today. Take the day off. He thought maybe Benny was hungover but by the tone of his voice he knew that it wasn't about that. It was about Lisa. She had called him very early that morning and she was in bad shape. She was having a breakdown. Jane. She had been crestfallen and needed to see Benny. Marco told Benny to let him know if he needed anything.

It was still somewhat early, but Marco didn't want to go back to sleep. His mind was in a fog. He thought many things as he lay in bed and none of them were making him feel anything but more alone. When he woke from the dream – the dream that could now properly be called a nightmare – he sat up in bed and began smoking. He had already finished the rest of the beer that he had in the refrigerator and he was drunk. Empty beer bottles littered his bedroom and the air was hazy from the cigarette smoke.

When he had gone for the beer in the kitchen he had passed by the picture of his parents and him at his graduation. His shoulders slumped and he almost collapsed to the floor in a kind of pathetic attempt at expiation. The picture judged and mocked him in a way that his parents never would have. He leaned heavily against the refrigerator door, beer clutched in his hands, and he thought that he would slump down and die right there and that would be the end of it. But his legs had not failed him and he returned to his bedroom and chugged beer after beer and smoked as if he wanted to kill his lungs in one nicotine-gorged sitting.

The room spun around him and the cigarettes were starting to make him feel sick but he kept smoking. He thought of the voice in his dreams. That fucking voice. He thought that he couldn't take much more of it. The voice had been right in the past. His daring to hope; his longing for even the idea of happiness; they had always seemed a dream all their own. Maybe the voice in his dreams wasn't a dream at all. Maybe his hope and pursuit of happiness were the dreams. Maybe that's what he had to accept after all.

YES.

Marco gasped and jumped in his bed. He looked around for the location of the voice. No, no there wasn't any voice. He didn't hear anything. He was only drunk and imagining things. It was the alcohol. It was the darkness of his own thoughts, that's all. He relaxed a little and sat back against the wall at the head of the bed.

You're starting to see, Marco. You're finally opening your eyes.

Marco's eyes went wide and wild and his face was one of pure terror.

*The truth, dear Marco, is staring you right in the face. The truth, sweet Marco, is now unfolding and when it does...*the voice faded and Marco hoped beyond anything that it was gone, but it returned. *When it finally does...it will be the end of you. And you will know that I was right all along.*

The room suddenly darkened and went pitch black. For a quick moment a faint yellowish light broke the complete blackness. Like a faint mist it hovered in the air then came down from the ceiling and stopped a few feet to his left, right next to his bed. His backpack glowed with the yellowish light and then the light vanished. The room went pitch black again for a second and then the darkness was gone and the room returned to a semblance of normality. He looked at his backpack on the floor. It sat harmlessly but it filled him full of fear. Slowly, he reached for it and set it in front of him on the bed. Before he opened it he knew what he was reaching for: the newspaper. He pulled the rolled paper from the backpack, his hands shaking.

As soon as the nearly month old newspaper cleared his backpack, a sudden, horrible shriek boomed across his bedroom. Marco screamed and covered his ears. The scream morphed into slow, echoing laughter. The laughter crept into his bones and he hugged himself with his elbows, shaking and terrified. Something that felt and sounded like heavy wind but wasn't wind shook the entire room.

Without knowing why he did it, Marco grabbed the small trash can next to his bed and he tossed the newspaper in it. He frantically searched his bed until he found it – the lighter! He pulled the newspaper back out of the trash can and clicked and clicked the lighter until the dry paper finally caught fire. He watched it with a manic expression. *Burn faster*! And it did. Steadily faster the paper burned and burned. When the flames were about halfway through the paper he tossed it back in the trash can and set the can right next to his bed.

The wind that wasn't wind rose to an explosive crescendo and Marco thought that his whole apartment would be torn apart. It roared louder, louder.

Then it stopped. And the voice began to laugh. *Do you think that means anything, Marco? You cannot run from the truth. The truth does not burn away.*

Marco was still trembling. His hands returned to his ears and his elbows nearly crushed his ribs. He was breathing harshly. Eventually he lowered his arms and he looked up. His eyes were huge and terrified. He saw it.

Standing in front of him, blacker than the depths of any ocean, was the Voice. It was looking down at him.

Claire and Dana had gone to work as normal, except they had gone in separate vehicles now. Dana drove the Neon and Claire rode her motorcycle. Claire had told Dana that she wanted some time alone to clear her head a little. Driving her bike helped her do just that, even if it was only for the relatively short drive to work. Dana was a little apprehensive but she agreed without argument. She would see Claire at work soon anyway and the two could continue their talk about what exactly Claire was going to do about Marco. She was happy that Claire was going to finally come clean and she looked forward to discussing it with her. Dana drove off first as Claire put on her gloves, helmet, and jacket. Dana watched Claire in the rearview mirror and comforted herself again in the fact that she would see Claire again in only a few minutes. There wasn't any harm in taking separate vehicles to work. They had done so plenty of times before.

The Voice hovered motionless in front of Marco save for the tendril-like inky mist that surrounded it. Then it moved – floated – closer to Marco and finally stopped two feet from his face. Cold, jaundiced eyes peered into Marco, unblinking. Marco sat petrified. The Voice had no mouth yet it spoke. In booming, gravelly intonation it said: *The truth has come to set you free, Marco, but only once it has consumed you.*

24

Benny was pacing back and forth in Lisa's house. She had called him very early in the morning, crying, almost begging him to come over. He did of course, and he called Marco to give him the day off; he didn't know how long he would be kept busy trying to console Lisa. Benny showed up to her house as soon as he could. When she opened the door he was shocked by how haggard and broken she had looked. She looked as if she had been crying nonstop for hours. She probably had been. She had an old gray blanket wrapped around herself as if for protection. When she saw Benny she gave him the most ghost-like smile that he had ever seen. The smile was forced and false. Benny hugged Lisa and walked with her to the living room sofa, saying nothing. He gently rocked her in his arms and kissed her forehead and dried her tears when they fell from her eyes. Eventually, Lisa looked as if she would fall asleep, and Benny half carried her to her bedroom. "I'll be right here," he said. Lisa was far away inside her head and said nothing. Benny quietly closed the door behind him.

Benny leaned against the kitchen counter drinking a soda without tasting it. He had no idea what to do now. He finished the soda and put the empty glass in the sink. He thought of trying to watch some television but he knew he wouldn't be paying attention to it and he didn't want to wake Lisa. She would come down when she felt a little better. He knew he couldn't just sit around though; he felt too restless. He thought Lisa wouldn't mind too much if he walked around the house a little to kill time and clear his mind. He went to the living room and absently glanced around: TV, leather sofa, coffee table. He saw artwork on the walls of a sailboat at sea, a woman sitting on a park bench holding an umbrella, a night shot of the London Bridge. Then Benny saw some photos on another wall and he walked over to them.

The photographs were mostly family portraits and vacation snapshots in what appeared to be chronological order. The first pictures were of Lisa's parents: pictures of them holding hands; dressed up at some party; close-ups of them together, their faces touching. There was a wedding portrait and some wedding photos. Benny still didn't know much about Lisa's parents, but from the little Lisa said they had sounded like good people and Benny would have liked to have met them. Lisa and her sister looked a lot like their mother and very little like their father.

The next group of pictures were of Lisa as a baby and then as a little girl. Then there were photos of Lisa's sister, Jane. Jane was her middle name. Lisa liked calling her sister by her middle name and rarely called her by her first name, at least not before playing with the sounds of it and giving her a nickname from her name. Her sister became used to it and thought it was kind of cute.

Jane's pictures were the same as Lisa's: baby pictures, school photos, party pictures, except the pictures now began to include both sisters. There were plenty of pictures of them together as little girls and young teenagers but very few of them as they had gotten older.

The last picture of the Cummings family was the one Lisa had shown him last time. Lisa had kept the picture with her constantly after her sister died. She must have just put it back in the last day or so. The picture of Lisa and Jane was secured in an expensive-looking glass frame. They were in a bookstore and they were smiling, hugging and happy-looking. They both looked beautiful and very similar, except Leesh had short-cropped hair raven hair that made a striking contrast to her very light skin and she had amazingly blue eyes. He wondered why such a pretty and lively young girl would choose to cut her life so short. Leesh. He had forgotten that was the nickname Lisa had given her sister. Benny had gotten used to calling her by her middle name. He remembered what Marco had said his new friend's name was. Dark thoughts crossed his mind. Strange coincidences.

25

Three Weeks Earlier

She felt the whooshing sounds of the electric glass doors closing behind her. The sound the doors made echoed sinisterly in her mind as she left the hospital in a semi-daze. She felt as if in a dream, as if she herself was not walking at all, but watching another person surreptitiously like a camera hovering in the sky. Alicia Jane Cummings had just confirmed the worst case scenario that she thought she had adequately prepared herself for.

She was going to die. She had thought it ridiculous and she had done all she could do to ignore confronting the situation as long as possible, as if denial or ignorance would change the outcome or have any effect on her medical results. But she could no longer deny or ignore the fact that something was killing her. She had a malignant grade IV brain tumor and it had metastasized, the cancer in her brain spreading to her spinal cord.

For too long she ignored the symptoms and told herself that they were nothing out of the ordinary and that they would go away on their own in time and she would be just fine if she didn't think about it. But the recurring headaches and the nauseating vertiginous spells she suffered kept breaking away at her false hope and her condition deteriorated further. She began to have seemingly random and terrifying moments where she had trouble walking and she had to find the nearest bench or chair to sit down on or at least a wall to lean against until she was able to take control of her body again. It frightened her but she kept herself in a shell of denial and told herself it would all go away. She didn't want to believe that anything could be so horribly wrong with her.

And she didn't want Lisa to know. She had been through enough; they both had. They were all that was left of the Cummings family when their parents died. Neither Alicia nor Lisa were married or had children and soon only Lisa would even get that chance. She didn't want to think about it but it was impossible not to know that she was going to die and leave Lisa completely alone. She had no idea how to tell Lisa that she had a malignant brain tumor, and worse, she didn't know how to tell her that maybe if she had gone to the hospital sooner there possibly would have been some real hope for her. But she had been afraid. She had been terrified and didn't want to put Lisa through any more pain and didn't want her to have false hope. But maybe more than that, Alicia knew that she didn't want to go through whatever treatment she would have been extended. The thought of going through treatments that almost certainly would do nothing to help her petrified her into inaction. But she couldn't hide what was coming. She had begun to sometimes slur her words when talking to Lisa, almost as if she was drunk. She would force herself to carry on a brief conversation, but it was only getting worse and she began talking less and less. She was having trouble focusing and she would forget things. Her vision became blurry at times which only further hindered her ability to communicate with Lisa or anyone else.

She became withdrawn and depressed and inadvertently became distant and cold to her sister. She didn't do it on purpose and she hated herself for it, but it made her tumor a four letter word that she would never say out loud. She didn't tell Lisa that she had gone to see a doctor.

The medical staff ran a battery of tests on her: MRIs, cat scans, a spinal tap. The x-rays of her spine and brain; the blood samples; the cerebrospinal fluid drained from her brain and spinal cord confirmed the worst: she was dying. After the tests were finished, she dressed and left the hospital, numb and in shock.

She zipped her leather jacket to protect herself from the sudden chill in the air. Her short black hair blew against her cheeks, wetting it. She had begun to cry. She got to her car and leaned back in her seat, biting a fingernail and tears streaming down her face onto her hand. She didn't bother wiping the tears away. She sat in the car for a long time, afraid to go home, afraid of what to do when she saw Lisa. After several minutes she started the car and pulled out of the parking lot but instead of going home she decided to go for a drive. She drove until she saw a CVS and went inside to buy beer. She came to a stop as she was passing by the pharmacy section. She saw the half dozen rows of little boxes and bottles lined up against the wall and blankly stared at them for a moment. The she reached a hand out and grabbed one of the large bottles and went to the cashier's counter up front. She paid for the beer and the bottle and went back to her car. As soon as she closed the door she began convulsing again. It was short but when it ended Alicia collapsed against the wheel and began weeping uncontrollably. Hot tears burned her face and a single thought kept dominating her mind: *I'm so sorry, Lisa. I'm sorry, sis. Please forgive me. I love you but I can't do this...*

She opened the bag with the beer and the bottle inside. She stared at its contents with red eyes and she felt as if she was staring into an abyss. She threw the bag to the passenger's side and looked with bloodshot eyes through the passenger window to something in the near distance. A few blocks away was a Holiday Inn.

The doctor had told Alicia that her brain tumor was inoperable and that she would need radiation therapy as treatment. The radiation ostensibly would target the cancer cells in her brain as well as her spinal cord. She had a grade IV brain tumor and the doctor told her that the treatment didn't really mean recovery, much less a cure. The severity of her condition was such that the radiation therapy might only be slightly delaying the inevitable and that the treatment itself might only be an exercise in making her feel physically worse without doing anything at all to kill the cancer that was killing *her*.

As she lay on the bed of the hotel room drinking her beer and staring at the walls, she weighed the options available to her. There weren't many of them and none of them were good. She thought of the side effects of the radiation therapy and what it would do to her body and her mind: the hair loss; the constant nausea and headaches; the crippling fatigue. Other than the hair loss it would be essentially the same thing that she was already going through. It almost seemed a better option to do nothing at all rather than willingly undergo getting cooked by radiation that would in all likelihood do nothing to help her. The odds of what could be called recovery towered massively against her. The chances that she would return to any semblance of real physical health were pitifully small. The likelihood that she would die frail, hairless, exhausted, and broken if she underwent the therapy felt like a certainty. She would die a shell of the person that she used to be. She didn't want to see or feel herself become that. She didn't want Lisa to ever see her that way. She looked at the bottle of pills on the dresser and she cried and turned her head to it strangely in an almost supplicating manner. She finished her beer and opened another one.

She had finished half of her 12-pack and was buzzing and her thoughts became less coherent and more desperate. She had become detached. She drank her beer without tasting it and continued lying on the bed with no feeling of the cotton lightly brushing underneath her skin. Alicia Jane knew what was coming. She thought of Lisa. She had to tell her that it wasn't her fault, that there wasn't anything she could do. *Please don't ever blame yourself for any of this. I love you and I've never meant to hurt you. Leesh loves you and always will.*

Her cell phone rang. She pulled it out of her pocket and stared at it as if it were some alien thing. She checked who was calling and saw that it was Lisa.

"Hello."

"Hey, Leesh, what are you doing?"

"..."

"You busy? I was just calling to see what you wanted to eat tonight. What time are you coming home anyway?"

"Um..."

"You there?"

"I'm here. I'm here, Lisa."

"Are you all right? What's wrong?"

Alicia shook her head as if Lisa would be able to see her but said nothing. She crossed her legs underneath her and stared at the bed sheets as if they were a most fascinating sight.

"Leesh? Jane, you there?"

"Yeah. Yes, I'm here. Sorry."

"What's up? You sound really out of it right now. Where are you anyway? You've been gone awhile."

The words came out of her mouth without her really intending them to. "Holiday Inn. I'm at the Holiday Inn," she said, as if that was explanation enough.

"Holiday Inn? You with some friends or what?" There came nothing but silence from the other end. "Hello?"

"I love you, Lisa." It was barely more than a whisper and Lisa could just make out the words.

"I love you too, baby sis. You know I do. What's wrong?"

"Nothing. It's okay. I don't want you to worry about it; it's not your fault."

"Okay...well we can talk about it when you get home. You're coming home soon right, Leesh? Jane?"

"Yeah," Alicia said, hating herself for lying to her sister so coldly. "I'll be home soon. See you, sis. I love you." Her voice broke on the last three words.

"I love you too," Lisa was just able to say before the line went dead.

Alicia finished all the beer except for one. She looked up to the dresser and grabbed the bottle of pills. It weighed heavily in her small hands. She tore off the safety around the cap and poured pills onto her hand until they began to overflow and fall onto the bed. She crushed all the pills that fit on her hand and reached for the last beer with the other. The hand holding the beer was cold and beginning to numb and the hand with the pills was beginning to sweat. It felt strange. Fresh tears were starting to fall from her eyes and rolling down her face.

She thought of Lisa and hoped beyond hope that she would not blame herself. She thought of the photo of them together in the bookstore, smiling and happy. Better times. Happier times. That was the memory she would take with her to the land of darkness, to eternal nothingness. She thought about all that could have been yet never would be. She got more comfortable on the bed and ate the pills in giant, messy, desperate gulps and drank the beer, and Alicia Jane Cummings closed her eyes forever.

26

Claire stopped at a red light and adjusted her gloves as she waited for the green light to give her the go. Traffic was surprisingly light. The only problem was that she kept hitting every single red light along the way, which was just as annoying as heavy traffic. Dana had probably already arrived at work.

As she waited more and more impatiently she thought not of work but of Marco. She would talk to him, even if it was too late. At least he would finally know the truth and she would have that burden off her shoulders. She felt finally prepared to deal with the consequences. She just hoped that she wouldn't lose him altogether though. Even if he did reject her romantically she promised herself that she would remain close to him. Closer actually. She would no longer avoid him if he called her. There would be no point anymore. The only reason she had done so was to keep him emotionally at bay. But once she came clean there would be absolutely no point to doing that anymore. No matter how much it would hurt, if he rejected her in one way or in every way, she would not lash out at him and return to her former darker self. Marco didn't deserve that.

She thought about the girl Marco said he had met and wondered if he would ever meet her – this Alicia. Her grip tightened on the motorcycle. One thing at a time. Besides, what could she possibly do to that girl? Beat her down? For what? Being attractive and good to Marco? She shook her head under her helmet and laughed to herself. She looked at the light, annoyed; it really was taking a long time to switch over. She might be late and get another earful from pasta breath if the light didn't change sometime that century. She hoped Dana would cover for her somehow if she was indeed late.

A vehicle pulled up behind her closely as she kept waiting. Claire looked in her rearview mirror and frowned, even more annoyed. The driver really was inching way too close to her motorcycle. Why the hell didn't he just stop next to her in the other lane? It's not like it wasn't free and he could have just...her fingers on the bike went white knuckle tight and her eyes went wide under her helmet. She froze staring in her rearview mirror in angry disbelief. Behind her was the blue Silverado.

Marco sat against the wall at the head of the bed. He hadn't moved from the spot since the Voice disappeared. He was trying to figure out what the hell was going on. He didn't even know what the Voice was; he only knew that it terrified him. It was warning him, but about what exactly? The truth? What goddamn truth? That he was losing his mind and seeing his own thoughts personified? Was the Voice even real or was his mind just becoming that far gone? Was there a difference...? The Voice...the thing in his room couldn't have just been his imagination; it was much too vivid, too...alive in its own dark way. Those jaundiced eyes, the inky black look of the Voice. The Voice. That didn't even make sense. Even if the Voice itself was somehow real there was no reason it should also be alive and in his face. It was just a voice...

But the shaking of the room...that had definitely happened, as well as what he did to the newspaper that was now little more than ashes in the wastebasket. It was as roasted and destroyed as charcoal after a barbecue and the smell of burnt paper still lingered in the air.

The truth does not burn away. That's what the Voice had said to him. Why had he burned the newspaper? What was he afraid of? *The truth does not burn away.* The truth...written in the newspaper? He thought about it. Why had he kept the newspaper? What was so special about it?

He tried to think back to that specific day. He had been hungry so he had gone to a fast food restaurant. He saw someone selling newspapers at a corner street and bought one. When he got back home he noticed an extra newspaper lying in front of his apartment door, apparently mistakenly delivered to his address. That's why that had seemed so familiar...he had an extra copy of that day's newspaper other than the one he burned to a crisp. Pieces of the puzzle were forming and starting to complete the picture. He kept focused on that day, determined to solve it all once and for all. He had eaten at the kitchen table and opened the newspaper he bought on the street and began reading the front page, then the sports section, then out of morbid curiosity, the obituaries...he had read the obits casually. As cold as it had felt to think such a thing, the majority of the deaths hadn't been exactly surprising. Most of the dead were older folks who had died of natural causes. The deaths of loved ones though, however unsurprising they may have been, are rarely an easy thing to deal with. He thought of his own parents and looked at the picture on the table. *Right, that's enough of that*, he had thought, and was about to close the paper when he noticed a final obit at the bottom of the page. The text didn't explain her cause of death, only that she had died at 25 and that she was survived by an older sister. He looked at her picture. The girl had shoulder length jet black hair and blue eyes. Those eyes, he remembered, had somehow stared at him through the newspaper beyond time and beyond her death. Beyond anything explainable her eyes had connected with Marco's.

Now, as he sat on his bed he remembered why he had not disposed of the newspapers. Why it had felt so incredibly important. He didn't want to accept what he had already known. Maybe if he never again opened either of those papers then that beautiful girl's death would somehow become not real. Her end would become void and she would remain living, somehow, someway, in some place. The girl would live, the girl he never knew and would never get to. He didn't know why he felt such a powerful connection to her. It wasn't just that she had been beautiful. There was something else that he felt united them in some way, a familiar darkness and loneliness that he felt to his bones but could not identify. And he desperately didn't want to let that go. His longing to figure out that connection, his death grip on that unexplainable yet powerful calling to this girl had somehow in the last three weeks locked away the knowledge that she was gone forever. That's why he had burned the newspaper. He wanted to cling to the final hope, the last tiny, dissolving strand of self-delusion that she was still alive. His mind had inoculated itself against the truth in a hopeless attempt to meet her – this girl he knew nothing about but for whom he felt such an all-consuming connection to.

The truth does not burn away. No. No, it does not.

Marco got off his bed and went to the kitchen. He remembered it was above the dish drawers. He looked up and he could see it. The end of the second newspaper he had gotten that day was just sticking out. He reached up and grabbed it and sat at the kitchen table. He unrolled the newspaper and turned the pages with shaking hands to the obituary page once more. She was there again of course at the bottom of the page: A beautiful 25 year old woman with short raven hair and eyes heavenly blue as any sky: Alicia Jane Cummings.

Tears fell on the newspaper around Alicia's picture and Marco hurriedly palmed the paper to dry it so he wouldn't ruin the only surviving photo of Alicia that he had. He stared at the photo with both hands on his lips as if to keep from speaking. The truth did not burn away; it was staring him right in the face. He covered his face as he shook and wept.

From out of nowhere, Marco felt someone's arms covering him, warmly embracing his shoulders. For a second Marco feared that the Voice had returned, but he knew that that wasn't it. The Voice was a consuming coldness. This presence was warmth. He kept his eyes closed and didn't fight against the new stranger's embrace. After a moment his shaking stopped and he gently pushed away and looked up to see who or what had been comforting him. Marco's breath stopped and he froze. Her warm, beautiful blue eyes were looking right at him.

Claire watched silently as the blue Silverado pulled up beside her. The passenger window rolled down slowly and before she ever saw the driver's face she knew exactly who it would be. Claire gave Dave a look of unchecked rage and belatedly realized that it was wasted underneath her dark motorcycle visor. She slowly lifted the visor with a gloved hand and wordlessly glared at him. The light changed to green but she paid it no attention. Dave then said something but she couldn't hear him over the noise of their two vehicles. She made no effort to try to understand and that seemed to properly piss him off more than he had already looked. She smiled under her helmet and didn't care if he could see her.

"We need to talk!" Dave screamed at her. At the sound of his voice she became suddenly aware about how much she now hated it. She deliberately shook her head in disagreement. There was nothing for them to talk about.

"Fuck you!" she yelled back at Dave and flipped him off. She finally acknowledged the green light and lowered her visor and began to drive away.

Dave floored his Silverado and immediately overtook her bike and cut her off. Claire barely managed to hit her brakes and swerve just enough to avoid smashing into the side of his truck. She jumped off her bike and ripped her helmet off of her head, nearly taking her glasses along with it. She walked up to Dave's passenger door and yanked it open. "What the fuck is wrong with you asshole!"

"I said we need to talk so we're gonna talk." He turned off the ignition and climbed off the truck and started walking over to her side. Traffic had finally begun to appear. A random car here and there drove by slowly, watching what they must have assumed was a car wreck. They slowed but didn't stop.

Claire scowled as Dave walked over to her. Ambivalent emotions kept her still when she should have sprung into action. Her cautious side urged her to jump back on her bike and speed away straight to work where she could finally call the cops on Dave and tell Dana what had happened. But the angry and proud side of her told her to run up to the son of a bitch and beat his ass, beat him harder than he had ever been beaten in his life. He needed to be taught a lesson about respect. But the push and pull of her thoughts kept her just standing there by the side of his truck, simultaneously a little afraid and furious beyond reason. She slammed his passenger door and waited as Dave closed the distance.

Marco was staring into the eyes of a dead woman. It was impossible yet he could not deny what was right in his face. Alicia was here, now, with him, but she shouldn't be. She was gone forever, yet she – or her spirit or her memory or some approximation of her, he didn't know – was right there with him. There was no glow or aura about her; she wasn't hovering in the air nor was she a translucent figure. She looked as real as the picture on the kitchen table and the sun in the sky. But Marco knew, as he always had known but had refused to accept; it was a facade.

Alicia's soft right hand reached out to his as if she was reading his mind and it was warm to the touch. That was no lie. Impossible as it was, he was holding her hand in his. Alicia smiled lightly at him and they looked into each other's eyes wordlessly.

At last, still holding Alicia's hand, Marco said, "How is this possible?"

"I don't know, Marco. I'm here and that's all that I know. I'm here with you. That's all I care about right now."

"But this isn't real. It can't be real. You're...you're gone."

"Yes, I am. And I am so sorry."

Marco shook his head. "No, please don't apologize, you have no reason to. It's not that, it's just that...I don't know. This just can't be real," Marco said again.

Alicia touched Marco's face with her other hand and then held it on his cheek, her fingers caressing his skin. She smiled delicately and tears fell from her eyes as she moved her fingers along Marco's face. "Do you feel that?" she asked. "This is real. You can feel my hand and I can feel your face. I can feel your skin under my fingertips. I don't know how and I'm not sure that I care. I'm only happy that we can. If this isn't real then I don't know what is."

Marco nodded, tears falling onto Alicia's hand. She didn't move it away. He wanted to ask her what happened to her, to hear it straight from her lips, but he decided that in a way it didn't matter. That life may as well have been in another universe entirely. Alicia was here, now, and that's all that mattered. Nothing else in the world mattered. He didn't know how long this moment would last or if it would ever come again, but while it was here he would cherish it and hold on to it with all his being.

Alicia's hand was still touching his face. He grabbed her hand in both of his and kissed it. They fell into each other's eyes and smiled. She was so beautiful. Marco thought about their meeting in The Majestic. It may as well have been in another epoch or another world. He thought that it probably was somehow. Alicia must have read what he was thinking; her gorgeous blue eyes seemed to glow in recognition and remembrance of that meeting. For the first time both their smiles were of unadulterated joy, devoid of any trace of sadness. This moment belonged to them and only them.

Marco stood, still holding Alicia's hand, and she got up as well. He put his arms around her waist and Alicia wrapped her fingers behind his neck. Her short dark hair fell across one eye. It gave her a mysterious, mischievous appearance and somehow made her look even more stunning. Marco bent down to Alicia and kissed her. Her lips were soft and her kiss hypnotizing. If this wasn't real then he didn't ever want to know what was. He hugged Alicia tightly to him and they embraced each other for a long time, slowly swaying together and almost dancing in each other's arms.

"I don't have a goddamn thing to say to you," Claire said. Dave was standing much too closely to her for comfort.

"Well I do. This isn't over until I say it's over. We still have some shit to talk about."

"What the fuck are you talking about? There's nothing to discuss! You hit me you piece of shit! What the fuck did you expect? It's over, asshole. It's been over. Now get the hell out of my way. You almost made me wreck you idiot!"

Claire turned to walk away but Dave grabbed her by the arm and violently jerked her around to face him. "Oh it is over you bitch. But only when *I* say so. And it's not like you didn't have that coming."

Claire ripped her arm free, fuming. "Had it coming? Are you fucking kidding me?"

"Oh don't play innocent," Dave said. "You can get the hell out of here once I hear it from you. Just tell me who he was."

"What? Who he was? What the hell are you talking about?"

"Who was the guy you were seeing behind my back." It wasn't a question. "I want to know who it was so I can beat his sorry ass. He can have you again once I'm done with him. You're lucky I don't do the same to you."

You've got to be kidding me, Claire thought. *You've got to be fucking kidding me*! Fury took her over and she gripped her helmet hard between her hands and smashed it right into Dave's face, destroying his nose. He collapsed to the pavement in agony, grabbing at his face as blood gushed out of his nose onto the concrete below. Claire kept the helmet in her hands. She was shaking from pure rage. Vehicles were passing by more frequently and some looked as if they would stop, but they must have changed their minds when they saw a man bleeding on the ground and an apocalyptically furious-looking woman hovering above him brandishing a motorcycle helmet as a club.

"You fucking bitch!" Dave screamed up at her. His face was a bloody mess.

"Fuck you, Dave. You have no right." Claire was stalking around him like an angry lion. Dave was covering his broken, bloody nose with the same hand that she had crushed with his Mustang door and this gave her an immense feeling of satisfaction. She smiled and shook her head dismissively at the pitiful, bloody sight of Dave on the dirty floor. Dave glared up at her madly and she saw him reach behind his back to grab what she thought would be some kind of rag to clean some of the blood off his face or try to stop the furious bleeding from his nose.

Claire wiped the smudges of blood from her helmet and turned her back to walk to her motorcycle, leaving Dave sprawled on the floor. She took a few steps to her bike, about to put her helmet on when she heard a loud noise that sounded almost like a truck backfiring. She felt herself grunt a little and she began to lose strength in her legs. The motorcycle in front of her appeared to waver, as if she was suddenly in the middle of the ocean, and her vision became blurry. She looked down and felt something wet on her riding jacket. She touched the wetness with both hands and her fingers turned red.

Marco and Alicia were still embraced and semi-dancing together when Alicia suddenly froze. Marco felt her tighten against his arms and he gently moved away from her a little to see her face.

"What's wrong? Alicia?" Her eyes had gone wide and she looked horrified. She was shaking her head back and forth. "No no no..."

"Alicia, what is it? What's wrong?"

She stared up at him, still shaking her head. "Oh Marco. She..." Then she shifted her gaze from his eyes, noticing something behind Marco. Her arms fell from him and she stood motionlessly staring at something behind him. Marco turned slowly. The Voice, dark as death, stood in the corner of the room. The tendril-like, black hole-like darkness smiled malevolently at them and said: *The full truth is here to set you free, Marco. It will consume you.*

Claire took another couple of tentative steps to her bike and stopped. Her legs were jelly and she stared at the red on her hands. Blood. She tried to take another step but her legs finally gave out and she fell heavily to her knees. She half-crawled the last several feet to her bike, leaving a dark red trail on the concrete beneath her. She leaned against the motorcycle and looked at her chest. Her jacket was soaked in blood. She put her hands weakly against herself to try to slow down the bleeding. She didn't feel much pain. She had gone into shock. Silent tears streamed down her face as she lay on the floor.

A shadow came into view and blocked out the sun. She looked up and saw Dave aiming a gun at her. He was smiling. Claire was crying but she no longer cared to save face in front of him. He couldn't defeat her; she wouldn't let him. She wasn't crying to plead for mercy from Dave. Dave no longer mattered. Claire was crying for Dana and for Marco. She was shot in the back and was lying on the street bleeding to death, and she was crying because she was mourning the loss of two of the most important people in her life.

She looked at Dave and the gun without really caring about either of them. She thought about Dana. She loved her more than she could possibly explain. They had been through so much together. They were inseparable. *I love you, Dana. I'm so sorry...*

She thought about Marco, her sweet Marco. *Things could have been so different had I told you the truth from the beginning. I'm sorry for being such a coward. I'm sorry for not trusting you enough to tell you what I thought. For not trusting myself enough. And now you may never know. Marco, I...*

"Drop your weapon!"

Claire looked to her left. There were two police cars and four officers taking cover behind their vehicles with their weapons drawn, their handguns and shotguns trained on Dave, who still had his gun aimed at Claire.

"Drop your weapon and step away from the girl! Now!" the same voice repeated.

Claire watched the action in front of her in a daze as her thoughts wavered between Dana and Marco. She looked away from everyone and stared down at her bloody torso.

"Sir, drop your weapon and step away from her now! This is your final warning."

Claire looked at Dave again. She saw the pitiful excuse for a man and she no longer hated but pitied him. She smiled weakly. Dave's face went feral and Claire knew this was the end. He would shoot her in the face at point blank range like the worthless thing that he was. Claire waited and didn't blink.

Except Dave didn't shoot her. For whatever reason, Dave spun around toward the cops and opened fire on them. It didn't last long.

Less than three seconds later Dave was riddled with bullet holes and shotgun blasts and he collapsed to the floor in a gruesome red mess. The gun flew out of his hand and he lay on the concrete before Claire, dead before he ever hit the floor.

Claire watched his lifeless body on the floor and felt less than pity now. Dave simply wasn't anymore and he may as well never have been. She heard the officers rushing over to her. She lapsed in and out of awareness and soon felt herself being worked on by paramedics. Darkness came and went and then she felt herself being hoisted onto a gurney and into an ambulance. Barely conscious, she faintly heard the wailing sounds of the ambulance's siren as she was rushed to the hospital.

The Voice smiled and the yellow eyes stared into Marco. The Voice no longer said anything, only came closer, closer. Alicia grabbed Marco's hand in hers and hugged him against her.

"Don't give in, Marco. Be strong. As bad as it is and will be – be stronger than it. And..." She grabbed Marco by the collar and kissed him. Then her blue eyes looked at him again and said: "And be stronger than me."

The darkness came upon them.

27

"What room is she in!"

"She's in the emergency room on the fifth floor. But you can't-"

Dana was already rushing to the room taking two stairs at a time. She was not going to stand and wait for the elevator to arrive. She reached the room and ran in.

"Oh no no...Claire!"

"Ma'am, I'm sorry, you can't be in here," one of the nurses said and gently but firmly ushered Dana out. Dana almost put up a struggle but that would have done nothing but get herself escorted out by security.

"Alright, alright," Dana said when she was outside of the room again. She tried to remain as calm as possible. "She's going to be okay right? How long will she be in surgery?"

"Ma'am, I don't know the answer to that," the nurse said. "It will be several hours at least. We'll let you know as soon as possible. Are you related to the patient?"

"Yes," Dana lied. "She's my sister. What the hell happened? They called me from the hospital but all they told me was that Claire was undergoing emergency surgery. What happened?"

"I don't have all the details, Ma'am. What I know is that Ms. Brooks was shot less than an hour ago and she's now in surgery. The doctors are doing all they can to help her, believe me."

Dana screamed. "Shot! Who the hell would...?" But she knew. "Dave, that motherfucker! I'm going to kill him!" She was pacing and crying, furious. "I'm going to fucking kill him. Oh Claire..."

"Ma'am, please try to calm down and not make threats," the nurse said. "We're doing all we can to help Ms. Brooks."

Dana nodded at her but kept pacing back and forth.

"Besides," the nurse continued, "vengeance won't be necessary."

Dana looked at the nurse with bloodshot eyes. "What do you mean?"

"I mean that there isn't anybody to take revenge on. Mr. Robinson was killed at the scene by police officers. He's dead, Ma'am."

"Are you sure?"

"Quite, Ma'am. Now if you'll please excuse me. We'll give you an update as soon as we can." The nurse went back into the emergency room with Claire.

Dana walked zombie-like to the nearest waiting area and sat down on a sofa, still trying to process what happened. Dave was dead. Good. Fuck him. But Claire was having emergency surgery and she thought the nurse hadn't sounded overly optimistic. She hoped that was only professional caution on the part of the nurse and not a cover for what the nurse actually felt about Claire's situation and her chances to pull through.

Dana was openly weeping as she waited but she did her best to collect herself. She pulled out her cell phone; she knew she had to let people know what happened. She called Claire's father but he didn't answer so she left him an awkward and tortured voice message. *Your daughter has been shot and she's in the hospital...That's a hell of a thing to be hearing about your daughter through a fucking voicemail*...Then she typed Marco's number. By chance Claire had given it to her. She never thought that she would need to call him, much less under the given circumstances.

Marco felt the Voice, the darkness, overwhelm him and Alicia. The whole world around him disappeared into a black hole.

And then...his eyes snapped open and he found himself sitting at the kitchen table, his upper body slumped over and his head resting on the wood of the table. He was sweating and shivering. His apartment was deathly quiet. The dream too vivid to be a dream had ended. The nightmare of the Voice was gone and he was alone again. Alicia was gone too and somehow he knew that this time it was for good. He felt hollow. Yet he could still feel the form of Alicia in his arms. She wouldn't come back, but he wasn't so sure that the Voice would not either.

He looked again at the picture of his parents. *Check out your son now, Mom and Dad...*

He thought of Claire and he felt a little guilty and wasn't sure why. But he had a heavy and bad feeling somehow. He got up and went to the bathroom sink to wash his face. He felt the vibration of the phone in his pocket before he heard it ring. He didn't recognize the number.

"Hello?"

"Marco?" a broken female voice said.

"Yeah? Who is this?"

"Dana. Claire's friend. It's about Claire. She's..."

Marco's heart dropped out of his chest and he felt his voice and his legs wanting to fail him. "What, what happened? Is Claire all right? Where is she?"

"She's in surgery, Marco. She's been shot."

Marco arrived at the hospital twenty minutes later. He saw the crying young woman in the waiting area who had to be Dana and walked over to her. She filled him in on what details she knew. Dave had shot her and he had been killed by the police. Claire was having emergency surgery and Dana said she wasn't sure how Claire was doing. Claire's father had finally called Dana back and was getting on a plane from Minnesota (He had been visiting his brother) and would be there before the next morning.

Marco and Dana waited outside the emergency room without saying much. There really wasn't anything that could be said. A few excruciating hours later the same nurse went up to them. Marco and Dana were white as paper. "How is she?" they both asked in unison, afraid of what the answer might be.

"She's out of surgery," the nurse said. "She's being moved to ICU. All we can do for now is wait. Her wound is very serious, but we're doing all we can for her." The nurse left and Marco and Dana continued to stand there, numb and quiet.

Claire's father arrived the next morning at three. He was understandably shaken and it was clear that he had been crying the whole flight over. The three of them exchanged quick introductions and they sat and waited. There was nothing more to do. Claire was in a coma and there were still no signs to indicate if she would wake again. This went on for the next week. The three exchanged shifts so that they could at least try to get some sleep, though none of them managed much. After the third week of waiting, Claire's father, Donald, more or less commanded Dana and Marco to go home and get some rest. Claire was his daughter after all. Marco and Dana went into Claire's room to hug and kiss her and then they both walked out of the hospital together.

"I'll walk you to your car," Marco said.

Dana nodded. "All right."

When they got to the Neon Dana opened her door but didn't go in right away. She looked at Marco as her eyes were beginning to turn red. "She loves you, Marco." She closed her car door and drove away.

Marco stood in the same spot for a long time, unsure how to process what Dana had said. *She loves you, Marco.* The thought made him happy but in a very distant, dislocated sort of way. It made him feel guilty too. If he had only been honest with Claire from the beginning about how he felt about her, instead of chasing ghosts, however wonderful such ghosts may be...But the words Dana said to him also horrified him, because he wondered if Dana only told him so because she thought that Claire may never wake up.

Marco sat on his living room sofa. His mind was a violent mix of conflicting emotions. He had stopped at a nearby gas station and bought a case of beer and was now halfway done drinking them. His pack of cigarettes was half gone. He got the picture from the kitchen and set it in front of him as he drank and smoked. His parents stared back at what their son was. "I'm sorry."

He was alone. A familiar darkness began to creep in and he had no will to fight it anymore. The alcohol proceeded to further darken his mind and he liked it. He opened another beer and chugged it.

And he thought of his parents and Alicia and how he would never see them again. He thought of Claire in the hospital, and he thought that the chances of talking to her and hearing her voice again might be about the same. And that meant the Voice was right all along. The truth had consumed and drowned him and he thought that maybe that was all right.

And Marco thought of fifth of whiskey and shell of shotgun.

The familiar darkness came up to him and enveloped him in its cold, dead embrace.

And he heard the same heavy voice mutter: *Enter night.*

Epilogue

It was an unseasonably cold fall night in the downtown area of the city. The streets were deserted and nothing could be heard save for the powerful gusts of wind tossing debris along the dirty, quiet people-less sidewalks. For a long time in this little part of the world there is next to nothing to be seen or heard; this little fragment of earth is alone and dead to the rest of everything and everyone else.

Then, barely audible at first but slowly building to a siren's call, something begins to drift across the night: six repeating notes sounded across the sky for anyone who would listen.

Acknowledgements

I would like to thank everyone who has ever read anything that I have written and provided feedback, whether it was positive or negative. It's all helped. Thank you to my family and friends who have encouraged me to keep writing. Very special thanks to Stephen King for writing On Writing and immense gratitude to Metallica, for your music, for existing and keeping me going through darker days. You're the catalysts.

About the Author

Jose Cantu is a lifelong Texan in love with reading, writing, narrative video games and anything that has a story worth reading or listening to. Energy drinks and passion keep him reading and writing long past sunrise. He lives in Katy, Texas.
Exit Light is his first novel.

To learn more you can follow him on Facebook:
Facebook.com/JoseCantuBooks

Twitter:
Twitter.com/LimitBreak323

Goodreads:
Goodreads.com/JoseCantu

www.ingramcontent.com/pod-product-compliance
Lightning Source LLC
Chambersburg PA
CBHW020248150626
46552CB00020B/717